DREAMS

The Complete Trilogy

I0583346

Book 1-Dreams: *A Peek into the Past*

Book 2- Nightmares: *Further into the Future*

Book 3- Reality: *The Conclusion*

Isabel

For Kegan- For helping me chase my dreams. I love you.

PROLOGUE

NIGHTMARE

I woke to darkness all around me. Everything was black. So dark, just like the deep depths of never ending darkness you would imagine that hell has.

Always night, only lit occasionally by the fiery pits. I would be grateful for the fiery pits of hell right now. Then at least I maybe could see what was all around me. But there was only the Darkness. The darkness engulfed me and seemed to swallow me whole.

Was that where I was? Was I in hell? It sure felt like it. That would explain the pit of dread that was starting to grow in my stomach.

I could see nothing. I could hear nothing.

I could not move, I seemed to be somehow restrained, immobilized. I could not feel my limbs, they were just numb. Almost disembodied. Since I couldn't see them or feel them, it's as if they weren't there at all.

I had no idea where I was or how I got in this hell-like situation. A situation where I could not see, move, or figure a way out. What could I possibly have done that was so bad I landed in this hell? Am I being punished? What did I do to deserve this?

I tried squinting to see, I tried to move my arms and legs and get a sense of what was around me, but no matter how hard I tried, I still couldn't see through blackness of this hell, and I still lacked the ability to move anything to try to get out of my current plight.

Pretty much, to sum it up my current situation, I was utterly and unequivocally screwed.

Just when I was starting to really panic, I finally started to regain some feeling in my body. The numbness was starting to wear off!

I wiggled my fingers and toes, confirming they were still there. Whew, yes all ten fingers and all ten toes thankfully present. But my celebration was cut short.

Something was moving on my neck. It seemed to be sticky, and it was dripping down the length of my neck. Slowly the sticky substance made its way from the top right side of my neck, right past the area on my neck that pulses the quickening beat of my heart, all the way to the beginning ridge of my shoulder.

I began to feel like I was starting to come to and beginning to become more aware of my surroundings, starting to realize where I was, and maybe how I got there. Everything seemed like it was finally getting clearer.

Suddenly, something tightened around my neck. Tighter, tighter, and when I thought it could not be humanly possible, it tightened another inch more.

The thing around my neck was rough and course, as it tightened I felt my skin start to burn from the friction of the object. I wanted to grab whatever it was, try to loosen it so I could breathe, but I was restrained, helplessly suffocating. I knew I wouldn't last much longer if it tightened much more. Once again a question ran through my mind, "what did I do to deserve this hell?"

As the thing around my throat continued to tighten, The air left my lungs and I could almost feel the oxygen leaving my body.

Then, there was nothing.

CHAPTER 1

THE MORNING AFTER

"Just Because you're burned doesn't mean you're gonna die! You gotta get up and try try tryyyyy" my phone's ironic alarm slowly started to pull me out of my nightmare. I tried to calm my racing heart and steady my breathing.

I am alive. Not dead like my dreams would have me believe.

This was the third time this week I had this nightmare. This week wasn't the first time either, this nightmare have been off and on for about two months now.

Nightmares had always followed me in my sleep ever since I could remember, but this one in particular really bothered me. It came without fail, while my other strange dreams were off and on, this one was persistent.

I usually could ignore my dreams, but it was getting to the point where I would rather lay awake in bed than sleep with the nightmare looming over my thoughts.

Insomnia seemed a better option than possibly dying in my sleep. I was really getting fed up with waking up terrified and unable to breathe. Each time I neared to end of my nightmare, I truly thought I was going to die.

Maybe it wouldn't seem so scary if I had any idea what was happening to me in my dream, it was just pure confusion. Every time I had the dream, I felt the same confusion and inability to be able to stop what's happening, an absolute utter helplessness. I never knew what was happening to me, and what it all meant.

Something was different this time though. Not only was I closer to realizing why I was there, but the substance dripping down my neck was a totally new feature of my nightmare.

My dreams are never normal. In fact when I hear other people's descriptions of their every day normal dreams, I can't help but be a little jealous of their naked in school dream, or their fanciful unicorn dreams. But hey, I guess that would be boring.

Who am I kidding? My life is boring enough without normal boring dreams to accompany it. With a life as simple as mine , I guess I should be thankful for the little excitement I get from my crazy dreams. Sometimes I even wish my life was a bit more exciting.

Realizing I needed to get on with my day, I had just started to stir and start to make my way out of bed, when I noticed something that happened in my dream was happening now-Something wet was trickling down my neck.

Was it the same something from my dream? No, that's not possible, it's probably sweat or something. I do run really hot, especially at night. Plus with all the stress form the dream I probably was sweating like a pig. Hopefully I wouldn't need to shower again. Ugh I did not have time for that this morning. I sometimes will get hot and wake up sweaty, especially when dreams are as vivid and lifelike as mine usually are. Even when the fan is on, I only sleep with a thin sheet, and if my dreams are bad, I wake up like I just ran a marathon. Not that I would a ever run a marathon, physical activity and I don't get along too well.

Or who knows, maybe I sneezed in my sleep. Wouldn't be the first time for it to happen. I swear my allergies sometimes have a mind of their own. I know most people have a allergy "season" but mine I swear lasts the entire year. No matter what meds I take my allergies just come back stronger and with a vengeance.

My hand went to my neck to catch the bead of what I presumed had to be sweat or snot running down my neck.

Wait- What the hell? I looked down at my hand to see it dripping with blood.

I hopped out from under the covers, through my bedroom door and ran to the bathroom mirror. Huh. I guess I scratched myself while I was sleeping.

There was definitely blood on my neck coming from some sort of puncture wound. I suppose that scratch could have come from my nails? I couldn't think of what else it could possibly be. Usually when I scratch myself in my sleep its a small scratch on my nose or something, never before like this one.

The really weird part was that once I cleaned the blood off my neck, the wound looked like a bite mark.

Pretty exciting for a Monday morning. Careful what you wish for.

CHAPTER 2

THE TEST

Though still a little shaken up, I had to begin my day. One nightmare and a scratch was not going to put a pause on my busy life. I had class in an hour and still had to get dressed, get some last minute studying in , and pick up my best friend, Nicole.

Situations like this is when multitasking comes in handy. I was packing my book bag, brushing my teeth, and looking over notes all at the same time. My bag weight matched my class load today, luckily pretty light. While, most days, my bag was heavy and loaded, once again like my normal schedule. This day was easy and light, only because it is test day in one of my classes, Theories of Personality. Its a psych course, and it is definitely not my favorite.

This course has changed my philosophy of acing or almost acing every course, to just trying to pass. This is our second exam, and due to my lacking and less than satisfactory grade on the first exam, a miracle needed to happen today.

The teacher was no help in understanding the material, he simply assumed you came in to class knowing everything, just like he did. I think he was naturally gifted with the knowledge of psychology and expects everyone else to possess that same knowledge. I swear he must have been born and immediately out of the womb he was quoting Aristotle and Plato. He doesn't seem to understand that we all do not possess such gifts. I am thankful if I remember to set my alarm, much less remember Kant's moral theory.

My phone buzzed, alerting me of a text message. I opened it and saw three messages from Nicole.

"Where are you, I'm ready!"

"Why aren't you here yet?, we're going to be late!"

"Hellllloooo Izzy!"

I still had to pick up my best friend, but luckily "picking up" just meant walking a few steps from my door and knocking on hers. She only lived a door down from me, we lived in the same apartment complex, so we often car pooled to school. If I was any later she would have probably tried to break down my door, so I rushed out my apartment and made my way over to Nicole's door.

She met me at the door, her whole self oozing with impatience. She was constantly on the go and often had to slow herself down to let me catch up with her. Nicole had long dark brown, almost black curly hair. I would get so frustrated because she would literally have it in a knot on top of her head, then as soon as she let it out her gorgeous curls magically appeared with absolutely no work. While my straight boring thin hair needed all the help it could get, and would never be anywhere close to hers. Her eyes she has always referred to as "poop brown' but she has these long eyelashes that most people would assume were extensions.

Nicole has been my best friend ever since I can remember, my neighbor, the craziest girl I know, and sometimes she acts as an overprotective mother. While she was all of these things, and so much more, Nicole was no help in the studying department on the way to school.

"Okay so what is Psychoanalytic theorist's vision of Utopia?" I asked with sincere confusion. I really and truly had no idea.

"I can't tell ya off the top of my head, I need the multiple choices then I see which one fits best. Hey Isabel, is that a hickey or something?" Nicole referred to the nightmare bite and succeeded in both changing the subject and making me drift back to my nightmare. I remembered the blackness of my dream and the weirdness of this morning. I fought off the urge to shudder.

"No! Who would be kissing me anyway? Come on Nic we have to study! I can't almost fail another test."

"You'll be fine. Anyway I made a B on the first one so I barely even studied for this one. Oh and I think Parker

wouldn't have any trouble kissing you!" I promptly
ignored Nicole and focused on the road in front of me.

The Parker she was referring to happened to be the
cutest guy I'd seen on campus, or really in the whole town.
He was all muscles, making you feel little in comparison,
with dark brown hair and hazel eyes that seemed to see
right past all your secrets. I have had a crush on him ever
since I could remember. If I had normal dreams they
probably would be filled with visions of him holding me in
his gigantic muscular arms, and me getting lost in his hazel
eyes.

Hell, a perfect dream would just be getting in a
sentence to him that doesn't physically or verbally
embarrass me. I can't help it, he just makes me so gosh
darn nervous. No matter how much i practice in front of
the mirror or rehearse our conversations in my head, as
soon as i see him in person, it's like I've never formed
sentences before.

I can just imagine it…Parker holding me and squeezing
with his uber manly muscles. I am by no means tiny, but
to him I would be like a feather. He could pick me up a
twirl me around, straight out of your favorite fairy tale. I
am all for a lady saving herself, but everybody wants to be
twirled sometimes, Okay? I can be a feminist and still
want to be spun around carelessly by a very muscular guy!
Wait, what were we talking about again? Focus, Iz.

As I pulled myself out of that little Parker daydream,
Nicole continued her rant by making kissy faces and

sucking noises the entire rest of the way. Which in case you weren't aware, is a bit distracting when trying to mentally study and drive at the same time.

We practically ran from the car to the classroom, seeing as we were late, like we always are. By the time we had scrambled to our seats, the droning professor had already started passing out the test booklets and was going over the test procedure, sounding eerily similar to a robot. As the ginormous test booklet landed on my desk my heart started thumping at a steadily increasing rate.

I took a deep breath and opened up the test booklet. Here we go, it's now or nothing.

First question of the test: "Pick which option best describes Utopia according to the view of the Psychoanalytic theorists." Ha. The irony of it all. Okay, focus up. I cannot fail this test. Think, think, think! What did Nicole say again? See which one fits best? I just stared at the paper hoping something would pop out or the answer would just come to mind.

The more I stared the blurrier the answers got, except for one choice. Choice letter C seemed to almost be bolder while everything else on the page was blurred. I went with my gut, or rather my vision, and picked C.

I went to the next, and the same thing happened. The question was, "Which part of the brain controls emotions?" Normally I would have no clue, but for some reason

Amygdala seemed to be coming out of the paper, coming right at me.

The strange eyesight continued the majority of the test, with certain answers blurred while others seemed almost 3-D popping out of the paper. I turned in my test and left feeling slightly nauseous, weirded out, and with a splitting headache.

I rushed out of class with my aching head in my hands and right when I looked up I ran into the arms of the cutest boy at University of Salemtown, Parker. My bag was empty, all contents scattered on the floor. Even with that embarrassing feature, all I could think was that Parker was touching me with his superhero arms. I shuddered at the thought, looking up into those gorgeous eyes of his, wondering if I could just stay in his arms forever. If monsters were haunting my nightmares, Parker Hunting was definitely haunting my dreams.

Figuratively, not literally. Stupid crazy ass dreams.

I first met him my freshmen year at Salemtown University. We were in a few basics classes together. Salemtown was a small school, so you actually got to know everyone in your class. There was never a question of where I would attend what Nicole and I referred to as grown up school, also known as college. I had always known I would be going to Salemtown. It's about an hour away from where Nicole and I grew up, but still far enough to where we feel able to grow on our own.

Even growing up in school I was never the rich kid, the popular kid, in fact I don't even think I had a stereotype, I just was a kid. Like I said before, there's nothing really special about me, then or now.

Not too any friends, except Nicole. Nicole was always the special one, in every club, cheerleader, in honors classes. Everything came so easy to her, while everyday I was the definition of struggle. She was the social butterfly, so by association I would hang out with her friends, but mainly I was a loner. Most people probably didn't even know my name, they just knew I was Nicole's best friend.

Nothing too extravagant about me. I got a decent academic scholarship based on my grades and dived at the opportunity to go to school at Salemtown. That way it could still be Nic and me, against the world. Or really Nic against the world and then I'm there too. But, since we had no control over class schedule, we were only able to match up in a couple of classes. That's when I first met Parker.

First day of classes, I was excited to learn, like the nerd I was. Then he walked in. The entire class it was all I could do to pretend I was listening to the teacher, when in fact I was trying very hard to not stare at Parker and come off as a weirdo.

About three weeks in, the dreaded partner assignment came up. Lucky me, I was paired with Parker. While he was smooth as silk, I barely could get out a stammer when I was around him. Luckily though my need for a good grade over came my awkwardness around the opposite sex and we aced the project.

So, now I guess you could call us friends? I actually mainly just still stammer and smile around him while he is the one carrying the conversation whenever we see each other. Every time he sees me from across the hall and walks over to talk to me, my heart skips a beat.

I nervously giggled as I looked up at the boy currently consuming my thoughts, "Nice catch," I said.
Pretty good line for someone barely able to catch her breath, right? I'm normally not that good at on the spot thinking so I'm really proud of myself for that two word sentence.

"I'd say it was the best catch of the day. Hey, Isabel Grace. " he answered and smiled at me with sparkling eyes and an equally sparkling smile. Only from Parker Hunting would my full name sound so amazing.

The thought of how he knew it barely crossed my mind when I realized I had not moved and was still in his arms. I awkwardly popped out and tried to gather my dropped things while trying to avoid those gorgeous eyes and those ever present muscles. However, my attempts at avoiding eye contact were thwarted when he reached for a dropped book at the same time as me.

A moment passed as our eyes locked, time seemed to slow down, and the breath was knocked out of my chest along with my heart thumping away ninety miles a minute.

I swear the book was about to slip from my hands they were sweating so profusely. My nausea that I had felt from the test only got worse. I bet the whole hallway could hear the gurgles coming from my midsection. Where was a tums when you need it?

"This for school?" as he grabbed the book from me, "Controlling Your Dreams?" His 100-watt smile faded as he frowned at the book. The spell broken, I quickly grabbed the book from him, and gave a rushed goodbye. Quickly thanking him for catching me, before I rushed out with the book in hand.

The book was definitely not for school, but one of my multiple attempts to solve my nightmare issue. But I wasn't about to tell Parker that. I had tried sleeping medicine, taking baths before bed, incense, tea, and every other home remedy the internet could come up with. He would think I was crazy person, maybe I was at this point, but I was really desperate. Heck, I didn't think half the stuff I was trying would work.

Nothing was working and this weird book so far was producing the same results. The book talked about looking at details that may seem minor and relate them to something in your life to discover the meaning of the dream. So far after analyzing my dreams, all I got was more headaches and still more terrifying nightmares.

There was still one thing from the book I had yet to try- a dream satchel. Partly because you had perform a sort of spell like incantation and that freaked me out a bit. But really, I had no other ideas, I was in the final few pages of the book, and the dream satchel was all I had left to do. I literally had no other options. The plan was to grab the ingredients, make the satchel, and say the incantation tonight before I went to bed, hopefully it will help.

The day passed by pretty quickly after that, my head still was reeling from my run into Parker. How can one person make my heart stop just by the touch of a hand? How can I lose my breath just from one look? Man, that boy has some skills. Too bad I don't have a chance in hell with him, like I said, hottest guy in school, and then there's me, no comparison.

When it comes to everything about me, I am pretty ordinary. I'm not too small, not too big, perfectly average size and height wise. My hair goes a little past my shoulders, bone straight, dirty blonde on the verge of being light brown hair. My hair lives most of its life in a ponytail, easier to deal with on mornings where I'm struggling to catch my breath from another terrifying dream. And hey, I am a lazy college student. Ponytails fit the persona. It is truly a rare and special day when I take the time to fix my hair, sometimes running a brush through it is its full extent.

My eyes are probably the most unordinary thing about me. I can't tell you what color they are, because every time I look in the mirror, I swear they change to a different color. One day they are forest green, next day ocean blue, then dark brown. No one else really seems to notice it though, so I just chock it up to genetics.

I rarely look anyone in the eye anyway. Other than Nicole, I keep to myself and keep my eyes and the rest of my thoughts to the floor and away from everyone else around me.

The whole rest of the day all I could think of was the dream satchel, and if it would work. Would it make my nightmares disappear? Could it help me have a normal life again? I soaked in the tub with thoughts of Parker, my dream, and all these questions running through my head. Even my usual trick of a good book, some bath salts, and a piping hot tub was not doing the trick. I sighed and reluctantly got out, knowing I couldn't put off the satchel any longer.

The dream satchel I had gotten from a local Wicca hole in the wall magic store still lay in the shopping bag on my dresser. It came already full of the herbs and stuff, I just had to anoint it with some oil I also got from the store. I figured there were two different outcomes, as I worked on anointing the little bag of herbs, either it would work and I would be free of these gripping dreams, or it wouldn't work and I would have to find some other hoax to try to put a stop to the nightmares.

I shuddered, thinking back to the weird lady who worked at the store.

Finding the local shop was easy, getting the courage to go in and actually figure out what I needed was the hard part. I walked in, took a deep breath and proceeded to the counter. Fully ready to state my rehearsed speech to try to find a solution.

Before I could though, the lady behind the counter popped out from underneath and said, "Trouble sleeping, dear?"

Wow, I must look like crap…I thought sheepishly. I always hate when brutally honest people say things like that. "Hey! Are you sick? You look sick?" Nope, just chose today to not wear makeup, thanks. Never making that mistake again. It's a great boost to the self esteem!

I shrug off her comment and answer- "I actually have had trouble sleeping…been having nightmares. A book I have mentioned something about a satchel? Would you be able to help me with that?" Whew. Rehearsed speech done! Now came the part hard to rehearse, the other person's part of the conversation…

She looked at me with pity, which I don't love. Yes, I have been struggling lately, but I am trying to do something about it. I hate to ask others for help.

I grew up taking care of myself mostly. Which is why having Nicole as a best friend is so nice- she's the one person who wants to take care of me every now and again. My parents weren't around much. I had a grandma when I was little who would help some, but she's long gone. It's really just me. But here I am, desperate and asking a lady who is probably looney tunes for help.

"I can help you find the ingredients, love, but remember with knowledge comes power. Are you ready for what comes next?"

She stares at me with such intensity, like I should know what the heck she's talking about. I guess that's on me for going to a Wicca store. They have to sell crap, so they put on a whole performance. Yet, here I am, buying the crap and hoping it'll work for me.

Finally, after what feels like the longest day, I am bathed, as relaxed as I can be, and all ready for bed. The satchel is anointed and safely tucked under my pillow, all that was left was to go to sleep.

Trying to fall asleep is the hardest part, since I know what happens once I do. Another terrifying nightmare, another restless night, and hell, maybe even another freaking vampire bite! Am I ready for all of that again? No. But hopefully the satchel and the book work. I feel my lids start to grow heavy, and I let sleep start to wash over me. Right before I fall asleep, I swear I hear a scratching at my door.

CHAPTER 3

DREAMING WITH THE DEVIL

It began as the others, dark as night. I knew not of where I was or how I got there, just that I was scared and in trouble. But one thing I realized quickly. This time I realized that there was light creeping in at certain pockets of dark, which made me realize: something was covering my eyes!

That's why I felt blind, my eyes were always covered! The same moment I realized this I heard mumbled male voices coming towards me.

"How is thee demon girl today? Has thoust given away ye soul?" Said the closest voice as he took off what apparently was a burlap bag over my head, shrouding me in sudden light.

I flinched away from the sudden brightness only to have the grubby, strangely dressed man grab my chin and yank it inches away from his smelly scruffy face

oozing pure hatred and disgust to me and whispered,
"Did we dream with the devil?"

I opened my mouth in response, ready to defend
myself, question my whereabouts, really anything. But
before I could ask anything or question my current
state, he smacked my face back into the darkness.

I woke up a start, fresh from the dream, still
feeling the man's warm thick breath on my face, his
grubby dirty hands on my chin, and could still see the
disgust in his eyes when he looked at me. I quickly
pulled out the dream satchel and tossed it across the
dark of my room.

Did it work? I'm not sure, this dream was
different, yet still just as confusing. At least I
discovered why I couldn't see all those times before. I
was blindfolded! It felt good to have at least one
answer to my list of questions.

But this dream raised a few more like: what
crime did I commit? Who was the man? Where did he
come from? Why did he speak to me like that,
referring to the integrity of my soul? Demon girl?
What does that mean?

New questions, but the answers would have to
wait till morning. I was done with that satchel for the
night. All I got from the satchel this time was me
getting smacked silly and more questions. I let myself

drift off again, but just as I started to close my eyes, I swear I saw a flash of white dash across my room.

In the morning I was able to think clearer about the dream than I had the night before. I realized that in a way the satchel did its job, it made me more privy to what was going on in the dream.

With my nightmare bite starting to itch, I thought back to what the book mentioned that maybe don't always consider the major things, but look at the minor details to discover the meaning of the dream. The major details can overwhelm the dreamer from seeing the truth in the minor ones. So with a cup of coffee and notepad, I began brainstorming little things about my dreams.

What we know:

*something was around my neck in the original dream, that's what constricted my breathing

*the man's dialect was strange, old English maybe

*I, or whoever I was portraying in the dream, was imprisoned for some crime

*he spoke of the validity of my soul and believed I dreamt of the devil

Okay, so I had some thoughts written down. That's it. Nothing jumped out at me like it had with the test. Then, there was also the confusing matter of my nightmare bite... Great, now it's itching again.

Exasperated, feeling, hopeless, and trying to think of something other than the crazy itching going on in my neck area, I turned to my relaxing escape. Books. Maybe even a bath and a good book would make me feel a bit better this time. Whenever I was stressed out and needed to get away, I would go to my books. A knight could rescue me, or I could rescue myself and the prince. I could become an underwater crusader, a beautiful princess, or I could develop powers and spell my way out of my problems.

The latest book I'd read had been about a group of witches, called a coven in the book. Most of them were still learning how to control their powers. In fact, the majority of them were in their teens and not only having to deal with the issues that come with being a teenager, but also having to deal with becoming a witch and all those new powers. Puberty plus powers, ughhh I am not envious.

Wait. Powers? Spells? Hmm. I got a sudden spark of high school history class and decided to follow my instinct and decided to do some research.

I went to my computer and searched several key words, 'historical', to cover the drab and the dialect. 'Soul' and 'devil', since both were mentioned in the dream, and 'powers', just because of the hunch my books gave me. After what seemed like hours but was probably only seconds passed, the results loaded.

Of the millions of hits, one event seemed to jump out at me, the Salem witch trials. The rope around my neck that seemed to only get tighter, was that like a hanging? Like what they did to women at the witch trials?

I read on to find out that just in Salem alone there were almost 150 people accused of witchcraft, and a little less than forty died because of these accusations. The "evidence" they claimed to have were outbreaks of illnesses, afflicted girls claiming that the accused cast a spell on them, birthmarks such as moles were also used as evidence, and if the accused had a pet or animal it was called their familiar. This "evidence"could lead to an innocent hanging to their death, being pressed, or dying in prison. People believed that the accused had traded their souls and made a deal with the devil, just like the man in my dream had said.

So a mole could send people to their deaths? I had tons of moles, freckles, and even a birthmark on my upper right shoulder, right in line with my shoulder blade. Does that make me a witch? Well, not now clearly as I am nothing but ordinary, but I guess back then a simple birthmark was enough proof to send a "witch" to the gallows.

Okay so now I knew a bit more about the history, but how does that help me with my dream? How does that explain why these dreams keep happening and won't leave me alone?

I didn't have time to really ponder the situation because I had a student teacher meeting with my psychology teacher, probably letting me know that I failed the test, and I rushed out the door.

CHAPTER 4

ALL SORTS OF MEETINGS

"Seriously!" I slammed the door behind me. That asshole really thought I cheated on his test! The whole conference was my professor trying to get me to confess to something I clearly didn't do. He had no evidence! Just his lack of faith in me that I could get every single question correct.

Hmmm... every single question correct? Now that I'm thinking it out loud in my head, which happens to be where most of my conversations take place, it doesn't sound very likely.

Well, one good point he made that wounded my pride was bringing up my past test scores, which weren't too hot. Neither were my homework scores, or my overall understanding of the class.

Well, Isabel the odds aren't looking too good for you. But I never cheat, even though I had plenty of opportunities I always chose a bad grade over cheating! I have morals! I barely even remember taking the test, all I can remember was the massive headache I had afterwards.

The more I thought about the evidence against me, the more I questioned my grade. What happened that day? Oh yes… I remember those beautiful big arms of a man catching me as I walked out of class. I feel like I could always trust Parker to catch me if I fall…

Okay stay focused! What happened during that test? How did I make not just a passing grade, but a perfect score on a subject I have no clue about?

I feel like the answers just came to me, but I doubt I could recall any of them now. Luckily, my professor didn't have proper grounds to accuse me of cheating, which is why he was so bent on getting me to confess to the heinous crime.

I was so pissed off, I didn't even consider how strange it was how well I did. Now that's all I can think about. All I know is that I'm not a cheater, at least I don't think I am. Yesterday I was absolutely sure of that statement now I'm not as sure.

Driving home, my overactive thinking was consuming my ride. All the events from the dream and the meeting were circling around in my head, making it hard to concentrate of driving. Which explains why I didn't notice when the stoplight turned green and I was still at a complete stop. I was too busy staring off into space, consumed in my thoughts.

A long honk and a "get off your phone girl!" Pulled me out of my trance. I quickly accelerated and then switched lanes to allow the angry driver behind me to pass me up. I looked over to see that he had not in fact passed me, but was cruising along right next to me, staring.

I felt this was a perfect time to defend myself, "Hey! I wasn't texting!"

"Well what were you doing that made you stay at a green light for thirty seconds?"

"Just thinking" I said, instantly regretting it. After defending myself and now feeling quite embarrassed, we both reached another stoplight. I have perfect timing in life apparently.

Now, we had a whole minute to awkwardly stare sideways at one another. Hmmm. Well at least if I have to be awkwardly stuck at a light, he's cute. His smile was what immediately caught my attention, it seemed to light up his big green eyes that were already lit up with something like mischief. He seemed to be built, but not too big, maybe some people would think he was too small, but I thought he was perfect. Perfect, like his sandy blonde hair that he brushed back from his face. I'm not normally this attentive to guys, or people in general, but there was something that forced me from looking away. I then realized I had been staring at this guy the whole light, making me feel like a complete creeper.

"So uh, where you headed?" He said. Normally I would immediately be creeped out by a stranger asking me this, but there was something about this guy that made me feel like I could trust him.

However, whatever my instincts were telling me, I was not stupid enough to tell him where I was headed, home, so I changed the subject.

"My name's Isabel, what's yours? " and of course my perfect timing returned and the light changed. He yelled "Zach Henley, look me up"!" Before he took off and then my unpleasant thoughts returned.

After the teacher conference, the confusing stuff that has been happening everyday all around me, and then the stoplight incidents with Zach Henley, I had to force myself not to pass out from exhaustion until I was safely home. I kept doing that thing while I was driving that always happens in school where you feel yourself slowly drifting en you have to shake yourself to stay conscious. Once my head hit the pillow, a guy with a great smile filled my mind, and a peacefulness came over me, then I was out.

Once I woke up, I realized two things: one, it was crazy early, the sun wasn't even out, probably because I fell asleep at nine o'clock, and two, I didn't have any dreams. It actually was the best sleep I've had in years.

Ever since I can remember, I've had these crazy dreams. This recurring dream had just been haunting me for months, but I've always been plagued with vivid nightmares. I never sleep without dreaming, except for last night. I didn't do anything different, I was super tired, but that normally doesn't make a difference. Then Henley filled my head again, and I was immediately relaxed.

Even my nightmare bite was more at ease when I was thinking about the guy I had only met for a few minutes. The crazy itching I'd been experiencing lately dulled to a random scratch whenever I thought of that random guy at a stoplight. Thoughts of a guy has never put me at such ease before.

I wonder if I'll ever see him again? I'm usually a nervous person in social situations. Even Parker who I've been crushing on for my entire college career, instantly put my thoughts into anxiety mode.

In fact, just thinking of Parker now crushed my relaxing thoughts, and put me on high alert mode. Since it was barely daylight, I decided to be proactive and do something useful and something I rarely do unless forced, go running.

However, to be clear my "run" is two parts jog, one part walk. Not in that order.

I "run" to the local coffee and sandwich place and get my favorite breakfast, caramel latte and tomato egg and cheese soufflé. Yes, it sort of defeats the whole purpose of the "run", but I feel as though they cancel each other out. The alternative is driving to get my favorite breakfast, and then I would just have all the extra calories. That doesn't mean I don't do that a lot of the time.

This sleepy college small town had few places open before 8 AM, but Felicia's cafe and bakery was always there for me. Much to my surprise this morning, as I came in huffing and puffing since I jogged the last bit, I wasn't alone. A bigger surprise hit me when the only customer turned around towards the door, Zach Henley.

I fought the immediate relaxing sensation that came over so that I could act like a normal person, "what are you doing here?" I accused.

He smiled that god awful, but really if I was telling the god honest truth, amazing, smile and said, "good morning to you too. Guess you looked me up?"

Embarrassment reddened my cheeks as I rushed to deny his statement, "no! Why would you say that?!"

"Why else would you be at my favorite coffee place at 6:30 in the morning?" He said smugly, his perfect smile twitching at his lips.

"What are you talking about? This is my place! I would have seen you here before if this was your favorite place." I gushed out, mentally going through all the times I have been here to reaffirm my recent claim.

"Guess you don't pay attention too well then," he rebutted with that smile erupting on his face.

Since I was too mature to start a fight right in the middle of a coffee shop, with absolutely no relation at all to the fact I'm horrible at comebacks, I huffed off to the counter to place my order.

Once I got my golden breakfast, I looked around at my seating options. Of course this normally would have been an easy decision, because I had a table. I had staked my claim on it for months before finally people stopped sitting there, or even around it generally. It's an unspoken common curtesy to sit at least three tables away if they are available.

This jackass happened to sit at the table right next to MY table. Do I keep my cool and pride and find a new table? Or do I demand he move over the customary three tables away? Thinking realistically, I realized it doesn't matter where we sit because the whole time I'll just be hyper aware of his presence.

Giving up, I huff over to my table, deliberately ignoring Henley. Much to my dismay, not excitement at all even though my heart started beating faster, he scooted his chair over next to me, fully breaking the already broken proximity rule. I glared at him, wanting to make him uncomfortable and forced to move.

"Sup Bel, " he said in response to my glare.

"Should I be creeped out by you?" I responded feeling more at ease the closer he got. This guy, who I just met yesterday and had barely spoken ten words to, made me feel more comfortable than I have with any other person.

"Am I acting creepy?" He said back, his stupid perfect grin poking out. Though there looked like there was true uncertainty in his mischievous eyes.

"Yes." I said immediately, before his face started to fall I quickly added, "but I'm not creeped out, should I be? You're not going to kidnap me or anything?"

He laughed and shook his head. This conversation was anything but rehearsed, but it flowed like we were reading a script. No awkward pauses, just genuine getting to know one another. We talked about everything from family, his and my lack there of, to politics, and even our dream vacation spots (mine is Ireland and his is Paris).

We were talking for what felt like minutes, but then I noticed other patrons were in Felicia's. I looked at my phone and realized it was already after eight and my coffee had grown cold. Whoa, almost two hours had already gone by. I glanced from my phone back to Henley, who all of a sudden was starting to seem uncomfortable compared to the relaxed guy I'd just been talking with the past two hours.

"Are you okay? Have the tables turned and now I'm being creepy?" I said trying to bring back his smile, but it didn't work.

"I need to talk to you about something...I wish we could keep going on like we are like nothing's happened but..." He paused and I wondered what we could talk about after knowing each other for a day that made him so uncomfortable? Was there spinach in my teeth from my soufflé?

"Do weird things ever happen to you? Like you wish for something, and it happens? Or you think hard and the answer just comes to you? Or do you ever have bad dreams?"

The last question he looked up from his coffee and stared back at me. I was shocked.

Who the heck was this guy and how did he know all this? I didn't know how to act. I guess he took my silence as encouragement.

"It doesn't mean you're crazy, in fact, you're actually pretty special." He smiled at me then, I was still too shocked to react.

"Have you ever thought that all these weird things, the dreams, the wishes, and honestly, you probably get headaches too…Did you ever think that they could all be related?"

"It's cause they are. You're a witch Isabel."

CHAPTER 5

KNOWLEDGE IS POWER.

That absurd statement brought me out of my daze. I grabbed my stuff and started towards the door, murmuring how I attract psychos. I ignored the crazy boy who was yelling out for me. I can't believe I let him waste two whole hours of my life.

I turned back to say a string of curses towards him about what he thought I was when I bumped into someone. Someone very hard and muscular. Crap. Seriously what is it with Parker Hunting and me running into his absolute perfect self?

"I feel like we've over used this comment but hey, nice running into ya," he said with a wink.

My hands started shaking as he helped me up. What was with my body around this guy? The total creep made me feel completely at ease and Parker gave me the shakes.

"I actually came to find ya, I knew that you love this place. I wanted to see if you would want to go on a date sometime?" He asked a bit nervously. Ha. I was making Parker nervous? I was just called a witch? What is this world coming to? Could this get any weirder?

I jinxed myself. I felt someone come up behind me. "Come with me Bel, let's go hang out somewhere." Zach was glaring at Parker, no sign of his usual smile.

"Hello Zachary, nice to see ya in town. You just get in recently? I didn't hear you had come?" Parker said with a sort of evil smile.

"Hunting," barely acknowledging Parker, Henley turned back towards me, begging with his eyes. While a part of me wanted to go with him, I just couldn't get over the witch statement. Also, I thought while I was standing there between two amazingly attractive guys, how do they know each other?

"We can start our date early if you'd like" Parker said turning back to me. I realized that being with either of these guys right now was the last thing I wanted. I pushed past them and left before they could stop me.

I was overwhelmed. Two of the most opposite, extremely attractive boys were just fighting over me.

I just got told I'm a witch on top on everything else. That's been my life lately.

I needed to tackle one thing at a time. It was strangely coincidental how I got told I'm a witch the same week I was led to the Salem witch trials. I can't be a witch though, I feel like I would have known sooner and not lived 20 years of my life as a normal person. A slight itch sensation came back to life as I walked over and started my trek back home. I looked at my fading scar on my neck. Where did that fit in to all this craziness? Did a vampire come in my house? Were vampires real? I knew that freaking out would not give me any answers so I gave up and just sat around doing nothing, staring at the television, til it was time for bed.

"Well devil girl, ye have anything to say in thou defense?"

The grubby man whom I recognized with terror glared at me with pure hatred. I was too scared, all too fully aware of my surroundings this time. I could see the angry mob behind the dirty old man, each and every one of them with malice in their eyes, each and every one of them looking straight at me. I was on a platform, hands tied behind me, restricting my movements. I had all my senses this time, unlike the other dreams. I could even see what was around my neck constricting my breath.

"Kill the witch, kill the witch!!"

The mob chanted in unison. I could feel their mistrust and pure loathing slithering towards me like a hundred snakes.

The thing around my neck was a noose.

"Any last words witch?"

My scream was the last thing before it went black.

"Isabel! Isabel! Open the door! If you're okay, open the door damnit!" Nicole's voice stirred me from that illuminating nightmare. I ran to the door and grabbed my best friend, tears streaming down my face.

"Shhh you're okay, Iz, it'll be okay, only a dream, love." She crooned as she patted my back in a comforting circular rhythm.

Nicole was one of the few people who knew about my dreams that had plagued me my entire life. That's probably the main reason she moved in next door to me when I decided I wanted an apartment after living in a dorm for a year. The day I told her of my plan to move into the apartments by our school, she started packing. I should have realized before that where I go, she goes. Not that I was really surprised, Nicole and me, we're a team.

She's taken care of me ever since I can remember. Bought me sprite, jello, Gatorade, chicken noodle soup if I was sick, reminding me to take my medicine when my allergies flared up, and been the shoulder to cry on when I had an exceptionally tough day. She Stayed with me after my dreams until I could breathe normally again, brewed me a cup of tea and made sure I always was okay. She probably qualifies as more of a mother than a best friend, but that's the way she has always been, I can always count on her to be there for me.

She's one of the only people who actually know about my dreams, how bad they can be. If I was a witch, would she still take care of me? Would she be scared of me? The thought made me cry harder, bringing Nicole out of the kitchen and back to squeezing me tight.

She loves me so much, and wishes I could see that she was on my side. She feels like I'm keeping something from her, but she knows if she asks I'll only get more distressed and upset. She just keeps squeezing me, tight, and she won't ever let me go if she could help it. She was thinking she could squeeze the scared right out of me and she hopes these dreams let off soon, she's running out of tea.

Hold up. Wait, What? I looked over at Nic who just kept squeezing me and patting my back, not saying a word.

She's worried about me, and wondering if I'll ever get through this. I jerked away from her and looked into her brown worried eyes.

"What did you just say?" I asked, begging she'd say that she was sorry, she was just thinking out loud.

"What are you talking about? I didn't say anything. Hold on I'll get you some tea." Tea solved every problem according To Nicole. A cup of tea wouldn't fix what just happened though.

I'd just heard Nicole's thoughts. I could read minds. This day just got weirder. While Nic was busy with the tea, I grabbed my phone and quickly dialed Henley's number.

"Listen, Isabel, I'm glad you call-" he started.

"Wait" I interjected before he could start talking. "I need to meet with you immediately- it's an emergency. How fast can you get here?" I gave him my address and attempted to usher Nicole out with repeated confirmations I was okay. She still was worried and wanted to stay and keep an eye on me.

Only thing that actually convinced her to leave was when I said a boy was coming over. I said we needed "privacy", she winked and left my apartment as quickly as she came, with dirty thoughts on her mind.

No that's not just speculation, she really was thinking dirty thoughts. Ew.

CHAPTER 6

BOYS, BOYS, BOYS!

Waiting for Henley, I was just alone with my thoughts. Luckily just my own since Nicole had left. How did that even happen? How could I hear thoughts? What else could I do? I have to admit, although the main reason for me calling Henley was to get some answers, the girl in me had an ulterior motive. I wanted to know what he thought about me, I wanted to read his mind and see what his thoughts were when he looked at me. Did he think I was pretty? Weird? Ya I know dumb right?

Here's the deal, I have to read his mind. Otherwise, I would have no clue if he liked me as much as I liked him.

I admit it, I like him. Even with the whole ruining of my naive life, I still think of him and can't help but smile, even though I've only known him for about a day. In case you aren't aware yet, I'm incredibly socially awkward.

I lack normal social skills and apparently make up for them in super witch powers. Yep. He seemed to like me, but I'm really just getting that from the way he smiles at me, but I'm pretty sure for all I know about him he could smile at everyone like that. Just thinking about him smiling at me makes my stomach flip, in a good way. A knock at the door caused my stomach to do another somersault.

I answered the door with full intention of demanding he explain everything to me and how he messed up my normal perfect, okay not so perfect, life. I was going to demand he tell me how this happened and what I needed to do to take it all back.

But instead I grabbed him and kissed him.

I had no choice you see, he looked up at me with those now sad eyes and I just became overwhelmed with a sense that I needed to make him better, take away his pain. This crazy thing happened though, he kissed me back.

Somehow we shut the door and made it to my small one bedroom apartment living room, all while remaining attached at the mouth. He had my face in his hands and my arms were locked around his back.

He broke the kiss and held my gaze with a twinkle in his eye.

Although it was only a moment, that moment seemed to reassure me of all the doubts I have had and will ever have in my entire life, one look in his eyes seemed to put me at ease. Then the peaceful moment ended and the kissing resumed. Not that I was complaining.

He pulled his hands off my face and then proceeded to pick me up, my legs wrapped around his waist. I felt like a little kid, even letting a giggle escape from my mouth. The giggle only seemed to excite Henley more, intensifying our make out. Things were getting pretty hot, and I think we both realized that one, we had only known each other for a day, and two there were more important matters to discuss. I mean hello, wasn't I supposed to be mad at him?

After a few minutes in heaven (haha, seven minutes maybe?) we were able to detach ourselves.

"I don't think that was the emergency you talked about, not that I'm complaining. " ha. Well, at least it seems as if we're on the same page about the kissing.

A twinkle was back in his eye and his famous smile was back on his lips. I nervously laughed and went back to my covert mission, trying to read his thoughts. Yes he just made out with me, but does that mean he likes me, or is he just a typical boy who can't turn down a good make out session?

I was intently concentrating for a few seconds, trying to figure out what he was thinking in that cute head of his, when I realized I probably looked constipated from scrunching my face so hard.

"Nice try, Bel," he laughed and grabbed my face gently in his hands. He softly blew a puff of air at me and once again his contagious smile slowly crept all the way to his eyes. "You can't read my thoughts, though you probably already know how I feel about you" he said shyly never taking away his hands from my face or his gaze that held my eyes.

I still was under his spell when I dreamily asked, "Why?"

"Because I'm a witch too."

CHAPTER 7

(UN)WELCOMED GUESTS

The spell he had on me, wait, don't say spell! Um the hold he had on me was immediately broken as I pushed away from his gentle hands. "What do you mean? How could you be a witch? I thought I was the witch, and plus, you're a boy!" I turned away realizing how sexist I probably just sounded.

He just laughed nervously and said, "Witches aren't just a girl thing you know, men can be witches too."

The socially awkward person in me stopped at the "men" comment, I still couldn't see people my age as "men" or "women". The most mature I could go was the universal term "guys" so basically I always sound like I'm from New York. Hey you guys! See those guys over there? Hanging out with the guys today!

See I told you, awkward.

I brought my mind into the current situation and realized how overwhelmed I was. I barely was accepting the fact of me, being whatever the heck I was, much less the cute guy (see there it is again) being a witch too.

"Hey I'm sorry but this is too much. I called you over here to argue a bit, then maybe make sense of the situation, and now I'm even more confused. I really can't deal with this right now and need to be by myself. " He looked hurt at that, but hey, he just threw the fact he's a witch in my face the same day I discover I am one; too much, too fast.

"Okay I'll go, but promise me you'll be careful. There's a few things we really need to talk about when you're ready." He said mysteriously.

Great, like that helped the already stressed out me. He gave me a kiss on the cheek making me promise to call him later. I went to my couch to seek refuge feeling empty now that he had left. Henley had a way of making me feel like I was home, and I felt so safe with him. But my entire world was in the process of flipping upside down and I don't think I could handle one more thing. Yes. I liked him...but did that matter right now? I need to figure out what the heck is going on with me. Adding another witch to my situation will only complicate things.

But I did have questions, and while google was doing its very best. I thought of someone else who could help me.

The creepy shopkeeper at the Wicca store.

She seemed to know that there was…more to my sleeping issues. In fact I didn't even tell her about my issues, she just knew! I truly don't think it was because I looked like crap either. What else did she say? It was super creepy and strangely relevant to what went down.

"With knowledge comes power. Are you ready for what comes next?"

I definitely was feeling some power, but I don't think I can honestly say I am ready for what is happening.

Did I crave something more than my mundane existence? Yes, but maybe I should have been more specific and wished for a dog or something.

I decided I would pay the shopkeeper a visit and without letting her think I am positively insane I would see if she could help me. But first I needed to calm down. Ever since Henley left I felt drained. The high that came from seeing him had gone and now I was truly alone with only my anxiety about the unknown.

I was in the process of trying to relax on my couch ready to turn on some mindless TV when I heard something behind me. Like a scratching.

I turned to look at the balcony sliding door to see a kitten scratching on the outside. I live on the second floor.

Suspending my disbelief how it got there, I rushed it inside before the apartment staff could see it. If we had pets we would have to pay five hundred dollars which I definitely don't have. As I went to quickly let in the kitten refugee, my scratch on my neck started throbbing. The white little ball of fur had one green eye and one blue eye and mewed at me when I picked the tiny thing up. I cuddled up to the kitten and it snuggled right into the crook in my neck. It then proceeded to lick the throbbing, itching, scratch on my neck. Strangely enough, the throbbing eased the more the baby kitten licked the scratch.

Still holding the kitten who I was now referring to in my head as Puff, I went to my computer to look more into the witch stuff.

I was still processing that what I was looking up, people with warts and green faces, was what I was. I am a witch.

Woah, I guess I have pretty good complexion then. I am never complaining about a zit again. That is a lie. I probably will, but I am thankful for the lack of warts and green skin unlike certain friends of mine from the little ole land of Oz.

Puff just kept on purring and rubbing into my neck. Having her there seemed to ease some of my anxiety over all the sudden realizations and unexpected knowledge I had thrust upon me today. I decided to embrace this sudden calm and try to get some much needed homework done.

After the teacher meeting, the butt hurt professor had been assigning more and more homework I think to find my weakness. I definitely had more work than the rest of the class did, I had checked with Nicole to see if she had the same workload. But, nope, all this extra work was just for me, just to make my cheating self come out into the open.

Every time I looked at the papers too closely, my head would start to ache just like that horrible headache I had the day of the exam. Even though I was dreading the migraine to come, I knew the work needed to be done. I also wanted to prove to the professor and myself that I hadn't cheated. This time instead of multiple choice like the test, this one was a free response type where the question described a problem situation, and you had to write down the diagnosis and the solution.

Looking down at the homework, after reading the situation, everything around me, the couch, the tv, Puff, started to blur and words began to form on the page in the first blank. There were even in my handwriting! What the heck is happening?

I wasn't even trying to use magic, and here it was. I felt like I was cheating. But I guess for the answer to come out of me, it had to be information I had retained at some point? I grabbed the textbook and looked up the disease I had diagnosed.

Gosh. I was right. Yes I actually did the reading, but I was half asleep at the time, and I didn't think I would actually remember any of it. Well, at least I don't feel like I am cheating now. I guess its like a photographic memory?

Well, at least that's what I'll tell myself to make myself feel better. I quickly went through the last two questions with my little mind trick, once again the answers appeared. I knew without looking them up they would be correct. However, even though the work was finished, the headache had just begun. Even with Puff nearby the throbbing drum in my head just grew louder.

BAM! BAM! BAM! Followed by a series of quieter dadadadada. I just chocked it up to the musical instrument inside my head until I heard a voice outside my door.

"Isabel, You in there?"

What? that sounded like Parker... I rushed to the door and looked through the peephole. Yep, it was him in all his glorified hotness. I opened the door and right when my eyes met his, I got a chill up my spine. He always makes me so nervous! He always will be my first adult crush I guess so thats normal.

"Hey," he winked at me "I got a text from Nicole saying she was glad I finally made a move and that you were expecting me?" he smiled expectantly. Although he seemed his usual attractive cocky self, something seemed off. Curse my nosy friend, she assumed when I said i was expecting a boy I meant Parker. I hadn't even had the chance to tell her about the new boy in my life, Henley.

"Um, okay. So what's up?" I said awkwardly. My head was still pounding and I was really not prepared for Parker to just show up on my doorstep. Puff started mewing incessantly, only adding to my anxiety and headache. Parker looked nervously at Puff and then back at me.

"Well, I figured we could go somewhere...You know, finally go on the date years in the making. Ever since that first group project, I have wanted to ask you out."

For the first time, Parker seemed a bit nervous. I thought I was the nervous awkward one? Confidence booster- I was making Parker, the steamiest guy I have ever seen, nervous.

Ignoring Puff, who was now full on hissing at Parker, and with Henley in the back of my mind, I agreed as wholeheartedly as possible with the current situation. We left my apartment and got into his ginormous truck. I had to literally climb in order to reach the seat. He still seemed nervous, but he also seemed like he was driving with a purpose.

"So I guess you know where we are going, cause I have no clue," I nervously laughed. My headache started to get worse when I got in the truck. He had this air freshener hanging in the dash and for some reason the smell was so strange. It was citrusy, with a hint of chemical, like nail polish remover.

"Don't worry, you're safe with me," he said looking over at me from the corner of his eye, keeping both hands gripped on the wheel. Did he just say that with a little bit of uncertainty? My headache had now intensified so much it was getting hard to see or hear. I don't think I could go on for much longer like this.

"I don't feel too good Parke.." then everything went black.

CHAPTER 8

THIS ISN'T A NIGHTMARE #THISISREALLIFE

I came to and immediately felt like I was in one of my dreams again, pitch black darkness, couldn't move, utterly alone, and without a clue about where I was. Without being able to see I tried to feel my way around, discovering my hands were tied behind me.

I was in some sort of chair, and since I couldn't move my legs, I figured they were tied too. I tried to loosen the rope around my hands with pretty much no luck. I wasn't the best Girl Scout, I almost gave my troop leader so many heart attacks. I clearly wasn't listening when we had the lesson on knots. In fact, when we learned how to strike a match, I was the lunatic who kept striking towards myself, nearly giving our troop leader a heart attack. Safe to say I didn't last very long as a Girl Scout. Hopefully I could fare better now…

Right when my eyes were starting to get used to the darkness and I was barely starting to make out some shapes, I suddenly was thrust into a different world.

It was nighttime, and there was no one around this time. No angry mob, no disapproving eyes, no grubby man spitting all over me, just me by myself on the same platform. Only this time I was dangling, hanging from a rope. Most onlookers would probably think me to be dead. I looked above me to see that the rope around my neck was tied to to the tree above me, it's large branches looming over me, almost shielding me from the dark skies. I stared at the knot that was keeping me dangling, and the harder I stared, the looser the knot became. The knot was slowly untying itself, or I guess I was untying myself really.

I suddenly realized that once the knot was undone I would go slamming down into the ground. At the same time this realization struck me, the untied rope simply lowered me to the ground, although it was still around my neck, I felt no pressure at all. I felt my feet reach the ground and then arms swept me up. I panicked, thinking it was the grubby man from earlier , or someone from the mob who had murder in their eyes.

Instead, I saw mischievous green eyes and a ginormous smile, wait is that Henley? "You came back to me." He said as his arms squeezed tighter around me in a lovers embrace.

"Isabel! Wake up! Please wake up, come on you're ok! I haven't even hurt you or anything.. Not yet... Oh! Come on Please!"

Parker's incoherent cries roused me out of my dream. Hey, the first pleasant one I've ever had. Wait, why has Henley in my dream?

Okay, not the time to think and analyze your dreams Bel, you have a crazy kidnapper currently freaking out in front of you.

"Parker! Chill! I'm fine! Well, I'm all tied up, but otherwise fine. By the way could you explain the whole tied up thing?" I was hoping this wasn't some weird kinky thing cause that's not me, not really into the whole dominance thing.

Parker finally stopped his babbling and stared right through me. I got a really bad feeling, please let it be kink thing...

He looked me right in the eye, "I'm a witch hunter, get it? Parker HUNTing?" I went pale all over and felt the blood leave my face. Man, I wish it was a kink thing.

"I'm not a full on hunter yet, I have to go through a sort of initiation first." What is this a fraternity? "I have to kill a witch." He glanced at me quickly then started pacing. Okay, not a fraternity.

Come on, I have been a witch for less than twenty four hours and someone is already trying to kill me? What the hell universe? Yes, I did secretly wish for more excitement in my life, but I was not wishing for this! I am not really sure I totally believe the witch thing either, I am still kind of in denial about the whole thing. I definitely don't want to get murdered for it! What is this the Salem witch trials or something?

I could tell Parker was freaking out, his pacing and plus he kept mumbling to himself. "Why did it have to be her? She doesn't have green skin, boils, warts, or any other witchy characteristics. She's cute!"

Um, thanks. Wow, the guy I have been OBSESSED with for years just called me cute. Is cute enough to not kill me? I wasn't going to bet on it. I needed to figure a way out of here.

I'm a witch right? I can do this. Maybe. I knew I needed to distract Parker though, keep him talking, before he did something we would both regret.

"Parker please don't do this. You like me right? We've known each other for years now." I was half trying to distract him and half trying to really reason with him.

"Thats what sucks Bel, I really do like you! I've been watching you and hoping, hoping that you wouldn't come into your powers. They can lay dormant for years you know. But they didn't, you didn't. And now we're here, now I have to kill you."

He looked at me, still looking incredibly attractive, but now his size made him seem menacing and scary. I was always hyper aware of his muscles, but now I was for a different reason. My life was on the line.

"My family has been hunting witches for generations, in fact my family was one of the main contributors durning the witch trials, kind of their glory days."

From Parker's thoughts came a photograph of his family from many years ago. In the center of the family portrait was someone strangely familiar to me. My mind suddenly flashed to a grubby old man, the man that haunted my dreams, add fifty years to Parker and they could be related. Judging from the photograph in Parkers mind, they are distantly related.

I now realized why I always felt so nervous around Parker. It wasn't because of some silly crush, it was because somewhere deep inside I knew, or my powers knew, man somehow even Puff knew, who and what he really was.

Back at my apartment, Puff was trying to warn me. A kitten is smarter than me, great. Okay, so what now? He was a hunter, and if I didn't act, I would become the hunted.

Parker was still pacing, but he seemed to be convincing himself of whatever he was going to do to me. Meaning that if I was going to save myself, I would need to act fast. If only I knew what to do?! Parker kept shifting his gaze to the table to my right in the other wise empty room. I looked over to the table to see what I was up against. A chill went up my spine as I recognized the object on the table, a noose.

He must have seen the recognition in my eyes. He followed my line of sight over to the table, more specifically the noose resting in the center.

"See, I guess my family likes to relive the glory days. Every initiation has to be done this way. I really am sorry but my family will kill me if I don't do this. It's me or you Bel."

I couldn't believe he was talking to me like this. Please, don't call me that like we're friends right now! You're trying to kill me for christsake! I managed to calm down and reconsider my options. So far my powers include mind reading, which Parker was just thinking babble and guilty thoughts, plus different ways of me dead, all bloodied, strangled, beaten to a pulp, head gashed open laying on the flor, okay that's not helping.

My other power was the one during tests and homework, all other answers blurry except for the right one. How was that going to help me? This wasn't a test, this was real life, or really real life or real death, depending on how it all panned out. Well I didn't have really much options, I hadn't been practicing long enough to be aware of other powers, if there were others. So I tried the test taking power, they seemed to coincide with my instincts.

Before, when my instincts were screaming at me to stay away from Parker, I didn't listen. Now I had no choice to listen to what they were trying to tell me, what else could I do? I concentrated, focusing on the right answer. How can I get out of this? The world blurred, Parker no longer was there, or the cold bare room, or even the table. But something on the table was still clear, the noose.

What? Is that some cruel joke? The answer is my death? I was still in intense focus mode, and the answer came to me.

My dream! I didn't die in my dream! I was hung from the noose, and then I woke up! Was that a dream, or was it a vision?

Wait a second Isabel, that's a dream not real life. How could I be sure it would work? But was it once real? How else could my dreams be so real, the grubby man was real, could everything else be real too? Was that me in a past life? Or was I just victim to an overactive imagination?

I feel like being a witch has taught me one thing, there's no such thing as coincidence. If someone has hunt in their name, they could be a hunter, if you pass a test that other wise you would have failed, it must be magic, if your cat doesn't like someone, believe them, and my dreams are here to tell me something. They're trying to tell me how to survive.

"It's okay Parker, just do it. " He came out of his crazy trance and looked at me. "You heard me, kill me. Better me than you, right? I'm making it easy for you, I'm giving you permission."

I took a deep breath and stared right into his gorgeous hazel eyes, "But grant me one thing okay? For all the years we spent what I had assumed as friends, don't kill me all the different ways that are running through your head right now. Use the noose like your family wants. " The mind reader thing definitely got him for a second.

He started walking towards the table that held the weapon of destruction, "Are you sure Bel?" I tried not to shudder at my nickname coming from his mouth. I wished it was coming from Henley's mouth, I wish I could see him smile at me one more time.

I needed to stop thinking like that, I quickly came back to the situation at hand and nodded and kept eye contact with my captor. I knew if the connection was lost he would go back into his crazy babble.

His hands grabbed the noose, his eyes never leaving mine. "I really am sorry." Tears started streaming down his face, I realized I was willing him to go on. I was willing him as he draped the rope circle around my head and into my neck. I willed him to tighten the rope. Even as my anxiety peaked, I willed him to keep going. I didn't know if I could will him to stop at this point. It was the combination of my will and the pressure of his family that kept him moving. My will alone wouldn't have been powerful enough. He picked me up and only then did I break eye contact as I finally saw what was on the ceiling, a hook.

I was still in his arms, still hyper aware of his muscles, he stood up on the chair I was previously tied up in. His hands moved to underneath my arms and we were face to face once again. Now, he was the one shaking.

"All I've been taught and trained is that witches are evil. They will kill innocents and take away our children. Kill them or be killed. Now I look at you and don't know what's real anymore. " Tears were streaming down both of our faces, as I went through every interaction we've had. Every fall he's caught me, every stupid joke we've shared, every group project we would race for the other to make sure we would for sure be partners. I not only saw our past, I saw a future flash through his brain. What he wanted us to be.

I saw the first date he really wanted to take me on. Us holding hands as we walked to our classes, I saw our first kiss after dancing in the rain, and I saw us kissing with me all in white and him looking handsome as ever. I saw a future that would never come to be.

Using the last bit of strength I had, I willed him to finish the job. He looped the noose around the hook, still hesitating to let me go. Once he did, all my weight would be hung from the hook, leaving me dangling and maybe breaking my neck, maybe killing me.

I wasn't sure of my next step, but I knew I wouldn't get there unless he let go. I closed my eyes focusing my strength, and willed him to let go. He was fighting me this time, and although my mind was stronger, he still only let go one finger at a time. It was down to forefinger and thumb when I opened my eyes and smiled at him. My hands still tied, but now in front of me, reached up to his face.

I stroked his cheek, "It's time Parker," and I pushed my hands against his chest, forcing my body out of his grasp and into the air. The last thing I heard was Parker screaming my name.

CHAPTER 9

THEN THERE WAS NONE.

I knew I needed to get up, get out, do something. But I didn't have any strength left. It was so much easier to just do nothing.

Enjoy the lack of pressure of survival, the lack of supernatural, the lack of difficulties that accompanied life. I really could do this.

Just stop trying, stop fighting what's inside me, and let the darkness that fills my mind take over. I'm always doing something to fight it, but what if I just stopped? For once, what if I just did nothing and let it happen?

But dealing with nothing is just that, nothing. There's no love, no responsibilities, no failures, no successes, just a void of emptiness.

I found a bit of strength from what awaited me once I awoke. My family, my friends, Zach, Puff, my powers, there was a whole new world awaiting me, but I had to face it first.

I willed myself into consciousness, knowing there wasn't a lot of time. Everything was blurry and not from my answer solving power. My vision was beginning to fade, just as the breath was leaving my body, I was dying. Really going into that world of nothing.

Being presented with that as my only option made me realize how much I didn't want that choice. I wanted life.

I wanted it even though the hardest thing to do in life is to live it.

I'll take it- I'll take the hard shit; I'll take my family drama that comes from parents who could care less about me; I'll take hard ass classes that sometimes I feel like I have no clue what I am doing in; I'll take this weird new thing happening inside me right now. I'll take the Something over Nothing any day. Guess it takes being on the brink of death to realize that. Oops.

Even through the blurriness, I could feel the rope around my neck. In my dream, I loosened it and slowly and with control, lowered myself to the ground. I had been in nothing world too long to have that much power left. I knew I needed to loosen the rope, I knew there wasn't a lot of time left. I had to do something now.

Even if I dropped hopefully I could walk away with just some bumps and bruises, at the very most some broken bones. Hopefully, nothing vital would be hit on the way down. I thought of the rope, of its knot and the sides of the rope that made up the knot. I separated the two sides and slowly loosed the death rope that was killing me. This time as I began my fall, I knew I didn't have the power or strength to slow myself down like in my dream. I passed out on the short fall down, not knowing what awaited me an if I would wake up again.

I knew this dream was different than the others. The other dreams have felt so much like real life, I think a part of me has always known they happened. I don't know if its some great great grandmother of mine sending me the dreams from her past, or if its somehow me from another life.

I was clearly in the past as I looked around me, seeing the tree I had been dangling from in my previous vision. But i was in my regular clothes from present day, and standing in front of me, in full puritanical garb, was also me?

"Is thou ready for what's to come?" The figure in front of me said knowingly. I for sure know she's not me, or not me in this life after hearing her speak. This is her time, and I am just a visitor.

I answer honestly, "I only have known I've been a witch for less than a day, and already may be dead. So am I ready? I'm not sure. But I guess the only thing I can do is take it one step at a time."

She smiled and said, "That's all any of us can ever do child. Witch or not. Taketh it one step at a time." She looked back at her Henley calling from a distance. Turning back at me and smiling she said, "I must go and so must you. Remember I am always here, and remember you are strong. Figure out who you are to figure out your power."

With that vaguely familiar statement, everything started to fade away. Huh. She basically repeated what the weird Shop keeper was telling me. I wonder if she knows more that she let on?

I awoke in a man's arms. (This experience has matured me and allowed me to be able to say man at least this one time) I immediately tensed up thinking Parker was back and ready to put me back up on the noose. I looked up and saw my savior, Henley.

He looked down at me and smiled, "Nice catch right?" I replied "best catch of the day," before passing out again.

CHAPTER 10

WHAT NOW?

Minutes passed and I finally came to, and realized I was still in Henley's arms, "Hey, uh, thanks, but you can let me go now, I'm good!"

He smiled at me sheepishly then carefully lowered me to the ground, keeping his arm around my back, steadying me. Although I could now walk and bear weight and was fully conscious, I still was really confused. "So not that I'm not really grateful and everything, but how did you know I was here?"

Zach smiled and said, "well, I can see the future..." He paused just long enough for me to look at him incredulously. Seriously I cannot handle more heebie jeebie stuff.

"Just kidding" he finished. "I went by your apartment to apologize for laying the whole witch thing on you so fast, I knew it was too much too soon. I knocked and knocked and I figured you were just mad at me and ignoring me, when I heard your familiar going crazy right by the door."

"Hold up my familiar? You mean my cat Puff? What the heck is a familiar?" I was trying not to get overwhelmed but it was getting harder and harder.

"Sorry, I forgot what all you don't know yet." He took a breath before explaining, "your familiar is your animal best friend pretty much. It always knows what you're feeling, and it can even out your emotions if you're freaking out. It also can eventually strengthen you and your powers, but because of the strong bond between you, it leaves little love bites every once in a while. " He then pointed to the hickey bite on my neck.

"Wait, what? Puff is what bit me? Why?"

"The type of bond between y'all is powerful magic, blood magic. It's the strongest type of magic to create the strongest bond. That's how Puff can always be aware of your emotions and can ease your stress when the powers start to go in overload. Puff is what clued me in on where you were. She knew you were in trouble and led me here."

He then pulled out a little ball of white fur from his backpack that I only just noticed was slung carelessly, open, across his shoulder. Puff saw me and then started fussing and scratching to get to me. Henley complied the prima-donna kitten and handed her over. Now newly covered with a few scratches, he shook his head in amazement.

"This is going to come off a bit trekky, but the bond between you is strong, young witch. But seriously I've never seen such a bond in such a young familiar, and such a new witch." He looked at me then and I couldn't tell what went across his face. Wonder. Awe. Fear, maybe?

Well, even though Puff and Henley had come at a perfect moment, I had already saved myself. I freed myself, even though it drained me afterwards, I was still feeling the effects. I needed to figure these powers out. I need to figure out what these weird dreams/visions mean. I had one while I was captured, that's never happened to me before. I've never had a dream awake, I guess that makes them visions and not dreams. Why was Henley there then? Was him coming into my life the same time I find out about my powers all a coincidence?

Finding out you're a witch, meeting a cute boy, then discovering he's a witch, finding out your crush is a witch hunter who then captures you and attempts to kill you, then finding out your cat is pretty much a vampire is all a little much for me for a while. I'll ask

Henley more about the dreams and more once I can wrap my mind around everything else. But one thing was still bothering me and couldn't wait.

"What happened to Parker?" I asked.

"After I caught you, I turned around and he was gone." Henley replied with a shrug. "He's such a pansy ass." He said in all seriousness.

Wow, Henley clearly hated Parker, which I would need more info about why later, I mean how do they even know each other? Now that i think about it, they seemed to hate each other at the coffee shop too. What does Henley know that I don't?

Even for all he had done to me, I couldn't bring myself to hate Parker. I had seen his guilt and regret for what he was trying to do. I could also read that if he had a choice at all, we would be on a real date, not a capture and kill kind of date. He imagined a whole life for us, and it was hard for me to condemn him the same way Henley was clearly doing.

I excused myself, claiming I wanted to be alone and went back into the room that could have been my death spot. I walked over to the table that was right next to the hook and noose. It was no longer empty, it had a slip of paper on it.

Written in scraggly, messy handwriting was a note from Parker:

I'm glad you got out. I'm sorry our first date had to go like this. I hope we can make up for it someday. You probably won't hear from me for a while, some people are not too happy you escaped. But I am. They are Not too happy with me either, failed my initiation. I'll be laying low for a while. Hope to run in to you soon.

Catch ya later Bel.

Hope to run into me soon? Was that a threat or a promise? What did I want it to mean? Even though he had terrified me, I couldn't help it. No matter what the boy had just put me through, I was still worried for him. From what I understood from what he said and from my brief look into his mind, his family was no Brady Bunch.

They seemed scary, like I'll kill you if you fail a quiz kind of scary. This initiation seemed like a pretty big quiz too. Alright Isabel, he did try to kill you. You shouldn't feel sorry for him. You shouldn't have feelings for him...

Did he really try to kill me though? I was the one who compelled him to put the noose around my neck. He didn't do it of his own free will. Still, it's probably not the safest idea to try to find him. What did he mean he'll run into me soon? Was that a threat or a promise? What would I do if I saw him? What would he do? Well. I guess that's a question for another day, because this girl needs rest.

CHAPTER 11

BESTIE VS. THE BOY

Two hours later, and I still wasn't asleep. See, Henley took me and Puff home, and who was waiting but Nicole. I didn't have to read her mind to know she wasn't happy with me.

"Idiot! What the heck happened to you!? I come over and the doors left ajar," I looked over at Henley sharply. He shrugs sheepishly.

"Parker isn't answering, you don't answer your phone, and now you come back looking like you just went to hell and back, with a cat and a guy who I've never met before! Hello, by the way I'm Nicole." That's my best friend, never missing out on an opportunity to flirt.

"Okay I'll start with the easy stuff, this cat is mine and her name is Puff. This guy who you are batting your eyelashes at is Zach Henley. The door thing was his fault, I think he must have busted it open trying to get to Puff."

I looked over and his somewhat guilty grin and tiny nod affirmed my suspicion. "The reason I couldn't answer my phone was..." Do I tell her? What do I say? Ha, I was kidnapped by my crush who happens to be a witch hunter, and oh ya I'm a witch? I may or may not have visions. I have crazy instinctual powers. And no I'm not crazy, and yes I know you were thinking that because I just read your mind. Would she even believe me? Or would she just try to cover my craziness up by giving me a years supply of tea? I looked to Henley for help.

"Okay, from what you can tell she's had a rough night. Let's leave it at that and talk more in the morning." Henley smiled and me and started leading me to my room. Oh my bed. I could really use that bed right about now, I feel like I've been awake for days.

"Wait a second. You may be cute and have an amazing smile, but I don't know you and don't think for one second that the tired excuse is going to work on me. I'm her best friend and have been for years. It's my job to protect her, and some new guy is not going to walk on in and-"

"Nic? Could you make me some tea?"

"What, really? Ya sure babe, coming right up. Just go on to bed. I'll bring you some tea and you'll feel better. We can talk more later." She finished by giving a death glare to Henley before rushing into the kitchen for some tea. She always just gets me tea, I never ask for it. So she knew that whatever had happened, it was a big deal. She just hopes I know I can talk to her about anything and she will always be there for me.

Yes, I had just read her mind. I couldn't really control anything right now, I was too exhausted. Her mind was on overload too, going ninety miles a minute. Her thinking about worrying about me, was stressing me out even more. So after she brought my tea, she said she'd talk to me in the morning and quietly left.

I looked over at Zach who was quietly standing in the corner, there if I needed him, but not wanting to overstep any boundaries. But come on, he was already in my bedroom, he had caught me as I was falling from the sky, and he knew I was in trouble when the only other creature who knew anything was my kitten. Boundaries are pretty much gone.

It's funny how different him and Parker really are. Not even counting the one being a witch and one being a witch hunter thing. Don't get me wrong, Henley is so handsome, but in a way that makes you want to get to know him and then he becomes more and more attractive every time he smiles at you, every time you're rewarded with his amazing laugh. Every time he shares a little bit of himself with you, you know you are going to fall and fall hard.

One thing that made me want to get closer to him was that fact I couldn't read his mind. Which was funny because earlier in the day, yes this has been a long day, all I wanted to do was read his mind. But now I just wanted the calm that accompanied the quiet. I know there's still so many things I should be asking, but I just needed everything to be still for just a moment. He seemed to read my mind, not literally I suppose.

"Would you mind if I laid down with you? Nothing else, I promise." A part of me wished there was more in his promise, but the majority of me was exhausted and craved the stillness his mind gave me.

"Yes please, that sounds great." Then with Zach Henley the witch on one side, and Puff the familiar on the other, I drifted off into a dreamless peaceful sleep.

CHAPTER 12

ZACH'S VIEW

It didn't take Isabel long before her lashes fluttered closed. I truly could watch her sleep forever. She looked so beautiful, so peaceful. I wish I could protect her from everything she faced and has yet to face. I wish we could just stay like this, with her in my arms.

Puff softly mewed looking at me as if she knew what I had been thinking. Heck, she probably did know.

"Ya, I know. We will have to tell her everything when she wakes up. I just want to give her a few moments of peace before everything goes to Hell again."

She had so much to learn and so many people who would be against her, willing her to fail.

She had lifetimes to catch up on and I would be there with her holding her hand through it.

Just like I do in every life.

I pulled Puff closer and snuggled up to girl who I had loved for my entire existence. Even if she didn't know that yet.

CHAPTER 13

PARKER'S VIEW

I know it was risky leaving a note. My family could find me, the witches could do a location spell and kill me. But I needed her to know I didn't want to end things like they were. I cannot believe things got so out of hand. I know I was supposed to kill her, but I want to protect her with ever fiber of my being.

She knows so little about her life and what it could be. I wish I could help her through all the changes and battles that are bound to come. I wish I could just go back to the way things were a few months ago. I wish I could take her on the first date of her dreams.

I look over from my hiding spot in the tree through her window. Ugh. Stupid Zachary Henley. Maybe he'll help protect her. I am going to need all the help I can get if my family goes after Iz.

She's on their radar now, no thanks to me. I swear I will keep her safe even if that means going against everything I have ever known and siding with witches.

She's worth the risk. She will stay safe, with or without me in her life.

END OF BOOK 1.

PROLOGUE

There was nothing.

No hopes, no wishes, no love. An eternal void of emptiness was all there was left for her.

Maybe that's all she deserved.

It was easy, simple; nothing complicated like what waited for her outside of the nothing.

There was no expectations, only the void.

Nothing to fail at, no people to disappoint. No eyes shifting away to hide their defeat. She felt like that's all she was capable of doing in the real world. Failing. Disappointing the people she loved. Constantly not meeting the expectations of those around her.

Would she ever be enough?

Did she matter?

In the void, she could forget. Forget what was waiting for her. Who was waiting for her on the outside...

She knows she is supposed to want to be present, to be with the people she cares about, to be alive...

But why is living so hard?

The nothing never expects much out of her.

But life…it takes and takes until she feels as if there's nothing left…

Maybe one day there won't be anything left to take.

Isabel reluctantly opened her eyes and stared at her bedroom ceiling.

Dreams had always haunted her, but lately its been something different. The nothing called to her. The emptiness flirted with her until she couldn't look away. The prospect of peace taunted her in her dreams. She was pulled to the same place that almost made her stop fighting to live.

But she had fought. Isabel decided it was worth it to keep living, and she was able to pull herself out and now three months have passed.

Three months, ninety different nights, but every single night was the same. She would find herself back in the void. At first, she liked it. Thankful for the absence of nightmares that normally plagued her.

But now, every time waking up felt harder and harder, as if her consciousness was struggling to take control. She never thought there would be a time when she would pray for the dreams.

Three months ago, she was normal.

Sure, she had debilitating nightmares that kept her from ever truly getting a good night's sleep. But with all she knew and was capable of now, Isabel was definitely no longer normal. She was a witch.

Three months ago, she realized the nightmares that had constantly plagued her, were warnings from the past. From an ancient ancestor? From a past life? She still wasn't sure.

Zach never wanted to talk about it either. Yes, he was helping her with her powers, or gifts as he likes to call them, but whenever she brings up her old dreams, and the fact that Zach, or someone who looked exactly like him, was in her dreams, he clams up and changes the subject.

Still, her dreams ended up saving her life. When Parker, her crush, and apparently a secret witch hunter, captured her, Isabel truly thought her life was over. But with an awake vision, she was able to compel Parker, and she figured out a way to escape.

Now, she was working with Zach and with the creepy but sweet enough shopkeeper, Valentina, multiple times every week to try to get a handle on her newly discovered powers.

Other than the visions of the past, Isabel has cognitive abilities; meaning, problem solving skills. Though, whenever she uses this ability, without fail, she gets a massive headache.

Does she use it to save the day? Yes. Does she also use it to pass tests? Heck Yeah, she does. Does she still get a massive migraine that takes her out for the rest of the day?

Yep.

But everyday her stamina improves. Zach claims she may have even more "gifts" that will appear as she grows as a witch.

Right now though, Isabel is taking it day by day. Hour by Hour. Minute by minute. Second by second. Everyday is a fight. A fight to learn about herself, a fight to control her powers, a fight with her relationships. Zach and her are taking things slow, until she can get a hold of her powers and who she is. Isabel misses Nicole, her best friend and neighbor, but Nicole cannot find out about Isabel, even though her friend can tell something is wrong. Nicole is still in the dark about Isabel, so Iz avoids Nicole altogether.

The only peace she feels is when she is in the void. But she can't talk about that with Zach...he can't know how much she wishes she could just stay there. Be apart of the nothing. Would anyone truly miss her if she was gone?

CHAPTER 1

BARELY HERE

"Psst- Iz…You nodded off again." My new friend, Elizabeth, from my Anthropology class scream-whispered at me, rousing me from sleep.

Ughhh. I have got to stop doing that. But its just so hard to stay awake. I feel so tired all of the time.

"Are you okay? Did you stay up all night studying?" Liz asked me as we leave the class. She doesn't know this, but I haven't had to study for anything in months.

"Yes," I lie. "My classes are kicking my butt." Also, not true. I have an A in every single class. Even though I pretty much sleep through every lecture. I read through the material once, and my weird photographic memory/cognitive power kicks in and the answer just comes to me. Literally. The correct answer bolds while everything else becomes blurry. Even if its a free response, the answer just comes to me. But then, I'm out for the rest of the day trying to sleep off my massive headache. I like to think they are getting better, but who knows?

Liz doesn't know me very well. This is our first class together and we definitely felt drawn to one another the very first day of class. The second her dark blue eyes met mine I knew we would be friends. I feel like we've known each other longer than the two months into this spring semester. It's hard for me to let her in though, since I can't fully trust her with my secrets.

I already deal with that with Nicole. Seeing her everyday and knowing I am lying to her is killing me. She knows it too. I wish I could tell her how I am feeling. Even if I could talk to Liz about it, just someone. I feel myself getting darker and darker since I can't talk to anyone.

"So what do you think?" Liz asks and looks expectantly at me.

I realize I definitely zoned out of our conversation. I missed some question.

"Uh...about what?' I ask sheepishly.

Liz sighs, not even surprised I missed her question. "Where do you want to eat?" She repeats, probably for the third time.

That's what is great about Liz, her never ending patience. Meanwhile, Nicole definitely would have screamed in frustration at me by this point in the conversation. Liz seems to know I am not at my best now, and I hate this is all she knows of me. I wish she knew me how I used to be.

"Want to head to Felicia's?" I request my favorite place.

"Sure," she says with a smile. "Should I text Nic?" Liz has the best of intentions, little does she know Nic is the last person I want to see right now.

If I let Nic actually talk to me for more than two sentences, she would see right though my shaky facade. She may even bitch slap me across my depressed face. She would say "snap out of it!" And shake me until I couldn't see straight.

Hell, maybe that's what I need…but it's not what I want right now. I need more time to wallow in my misery. My nothingness. I also should be able to save myself, right?

Nicole would see me in my void and try to pull me out with me kicking and screaming. She loves me too much to let me suffer. But I really need to figure out how to pull myself out of this…

"Uh, she actually has a test later. Let's just head that way and maybe she can catch us after." I quickly lied to appease Liz.

Yes. I was avoiding Nicole. Liz is safe and won't push me to my limits, but I know she's worried about me too.

I'm worried about me.

The next hour drags on and even my favorite breakfast at my favorite cafe does nothing to pull me out of my funk. Liz kept the conversation moving, but it wasn't til she left that I realized I had no idea what we had been talking about for the past hour.

Who knows how long I was by myself in the booth before I realized I was alone again? Too long for comfort, that's for sure.

I look down at my phone and see three missed calls and ten text messages. One call and two texts were from Nicole, her weird spidey sense probably letting her know something's up, and the rest of the alerts were all from Zach Henley.

"Hey! Need me to pick you up?"
"Hey, you close?"
"Where are you?"
"Iz...all good?"
"Hellooooo"

There were a few more like that, and each one seemed to get more progressively frantic. I completely forgot I was supposed to meet Zach and Valentina today, uhhh forty minutes ago...Oops. I grabbed my bag and ran out of the booth, hoping Zach wouldn't be too freaked out at my lateness.

CHAPTER 2

FAILING UPHILL

I remember the first time I walked into the magic shop. I was so naive and unprepared for what was headed my way,

Now, the shriveled animal body parts, dried poisonous plants, and cauldrons of all shapes and sizes do not even phase me as I enter the store. *Ding Dong*!

"I'm sorry! I just completely lost track of time..." I quickly state as Zach comes rushing at me. He is so close his nervous breathing is tickling my lashes.

I take a step back and put some much needed space between us. My body craves his, but my body and my brain aren't on the same page at the moment...

The second he enters the room my body immediately responds. Trying to inch towards him, my normally fuzzled brain feels a little clearer with him around.

Ughh it feels like cheating! I want to fix myself without Nicole, without Puff, and without Zachary Henley!

I hurriedly cross the room to Valentina who stands patiently behind the counter. I avoid looking at Zach, knowing he probably has a look of heartbreak across his handsome face.

"Are you ready, dear?" Valentina says with a knowing smile.

"As I'll ever be." I answer with a forced grin. I know I need these lessons, but so far they just result in more headaches and more confusion about the extent of my powers.

I look across the counter to see what will likely by my mission today. I see a large feather, a rock the size of my head, and a single bead on the glass countertop.

Whatever we're testing today, I know it probably won't end well…

"I want you to stack the items" Valentina states. Hmmm okay that's not too bad.

Bracing myself for a gnarly headache, I levitate the feather, forcing it to rest upon the rock. Whew. Halfway there.

I feel the tension rising from my shoulders to my neck. Making sure the feather is balanced just right, I move on to the plastic bead. The red bead reminds me of my childhood, specifically my friendship bracelets with Nicole. It reminds me of simpler times. I quickly set it up on the feather, careful not to upset the balance, and clearing my mind of anything that may cause me to burst into unnecessary tears. I looked to Valentina, triumphant.

She looked to my pile, shook her head, and said with her annoying, knowing smile, "You didn't let me finish...I want the bead on bottom, feather in the middle, and the rock on top."

I almost walk out right then and there. Anger pulsating through my veins. Zach comes out from behind me and sweeps a hand across my first pile. The rock, feather, and bead now spaced apart evenly, just as they began.

I spare a glance his way, knowing I shouldn't. He doesn't even seem tired! How does he effortlessly conduct magic while I feel like I just ran a 5K?! Not that I would EVER run a 5K, unless I was held at gunpoint. That is besides the freaking point! I let out a "humph" and angle my body away from him.

Moving the bead and feather take no time, in fact, I may have even rushed it, trying to show off a little after Zach's annoying show off.

But as I glanced at the rock, my exhaustion was very much showing. Sweat was glistening on my forehead. I am not the type who can casually work out and barely break a sweat. My entire body shines and I become a tomato. I am NOT exaggerating, my face gets red and puffy and shiny…a full on tomato, just ripe for the picking.

As I lifted the rock mentally, my hands felt as though they were shaking. Or maybe my eyes were?

"Take a breath, Isabel or your control will slip," Valentina warned.

I then realized I wasn't the one shaking, the rock was. The twenty pound rock the size of my head was shaking as it floated above the shiny glass countertop.

"Iz, do you need my-" Zach interjected; leaning in as if to try to save the day, once again.

"NO." I screamed, and the rock fell into the glass counter, shattering the very surface it was meant to balance above.

I tried to grab the rock with my hands, trying to slow its fall, and in doing so, shards of glass brushed against my skin. I looked in shock at my now bloody hand, covered in tiny cuts.

I felt Zach and Valentina's desire to help me, to fix me, but I couldn't take it another second. I ran out the side door Valentina mainly uses for deliveries and smoke breaks. (Not cigarette smoke breaks, literally fire breaks from all the things she's constantly burning.)

I lean against the brick wall trying to catch my breath. I just tried to rush myself, that's all. Ever since almost dying, I constantly feel the need to try and prove myself to everyone around me. Yes, I did save myself that day...but in the end, Zach still had to literally catch me from falling out of the sky. I was too weak. I'm barely strong enough to pull myself out of the void every morning. Just like now with this stupid rock, I am too weak.

In through the nose, and out through the mouth. In for four beats, and out for eight...Okay. Better. What's next?

Okay, something I can see- a dirty brick wall with gum and who knows what stuck to the exterior.

Something I can hear- cars whizzing by on the block in front of Valentina's shop.

Okay, almost there- smell. Honestly, smells like pee. From what? I do not want to know. Hopefully it's just cat pee...

Taste is the hard one, as I feel like its been hours since I have eaten. I think back to what I had at the cafe, of the cheesy egg soufflé that I crave every morning.

Touch-okay gross. There is almost a slime coming off of this brick wall, but okay, what can I touch? To avoid touching anything around me, I absentmindedly rub my arms up and down, trying to comfort myself all the while fulfilling my sense list.

Breathing and Senses checklist...all of my calming techniques are out today!

They are working though, so maybe it was worth the YouTube playlist and multiple yoga classes. I feel my heart rate calming down, when I sense someone watching me.

Thinking Henley followed me out here, I whip around ready to yell. But no one is there.

Huh. Guess my almost panic attack has me on edge. I take one more deep breath, almost ready to go back inside and help clean up the mess I made.

I swear I smell men's cologne follow me as I make my way inside.

CHAPTER 3

AVOIDANCE

"I wish you would take it a little easier on yourself, Iz."

Zach Henley was walking me back to my apartment, at his insistence I shouldn't be alone.

He currently was trying to comfort me after several failed attempts including a broken countertop, several abused feathers, and beads beaten to bits. I definitely was ringing up a tab over at Valentina's with all this destroyed merchandise.

"You can't compare us, Iz. I have been training my whole existence for this." I hate when he talks like that, like everything is life or death. When in actuality, most days are just about the day to day normal moments. Did I finish all my homework for anthropology? Do I need to go grocery shopping tomorrow? Did I remember to brush my teeth this morning? Wait...Did I? Let's go with yes.

"I am trying hard not to, I just hate failing." I told him the truth. I really do hate failing. I am a perfectionist people pleaser and so this magic stuff has been a real slap in the face to my ego.

"You're not failing, you're learning. You're... you're just incredible, Isabel." Henley stops and just looks at me, waiting, waiting for me to do something, say something.

"I..uh, thanks. You are cool too, Zach." Ugh. Cool? That's all I can say to the most perfect guy? He truly is the sweetest, and sometimes he is the easiest to be around, and other times I struggle to speak around him like a normal person!

I look around to see we are approaching my apartment. I awkwardly wave and give him the one-armed side hug before full on running away from continuing this conversation.

Pretty mature, Isabel Grace. Way to go. You really won that conversation. Now he will totally want to date you.

Honestly, I can't even focus on my feelings (or lack there of; I am staying open to all possibilities) for Henley right now, when I can barely handle how I feel about myself.

That's probably another reason this magic stuff has been so tough. I'm not...right at the moment. I need to figure out what's going on in my head.

Puff meows at me desperately. How dare I walk in and not immediately drop everything to pet her? The insolence!

Puff is my familiar and though I don't think I can exactly read her thoughts, I definitely can get a sense of what she's thinking.

Is that because she's my familiar and we have a deep connection? Or is it because mind reading is one of my powers? Who knows? Either way I am definitely getting some angry cat vibes from my little ball of white fur.

I reach down to pet her before she decides to take revenge on me by scratching up my leather futon. Hopefully its not too late, I was gone longer than I thought I would be...

Avoiding thoughts of ruined leather, I absentmindedly scratch Puff's head while I mentally obsess about what just happened at the magic shop.

I bet without Zach and Valentina watching me I could do it. Maybe it was just the pressure of performing on cue? I look around my cluttered, but clean apartment to see what I could experiment with.

I live in a small one bedroom, and pretty much its full of books. My one splurge is my book shelf that consumes my living room. Books fill the wall, ranging from fantasy to self help, to now a sprinkling of witch lore. I realized a few months ago that the internet had limited knowledge of my condition...

I find the smallest book I can find, a little book of poetry Nicole gave me when we graduated high school.

"Here's a little book to help when you run out of things to say and are a little lost. Ask the greats what to do." Nicole often spoke for me growing up. She always knew exactly what I wanted and needed. If she only knew how many times through the years I asked Langston Hughes for advice. Whenever I would struggle, whether its school, or my lack of communication with my family, I flipped the pages and landed on a random poem. Most of the time I was instantly inspired and ready to conquer the world.

Right now though, there is a thin layer of dust around my trusty little book. I haven't consulted the greats in a while.

I grab a hair clip and the heaviest textbook in my bag. The one class that enforces the "buy the book" policy, instead of just having it digitally. Statistics. Ugh.

I lay the hair clip on my coffee table, letting Puff sulk off to her bed due to lack of pets. I put the textbook next to it and the little book of poetry on its other side.

Take a breath. Focus on what you're about to do. First, the book. Concentrating my energy on the small little book that makes me think of my best friend, I willed it to rise above the table. I moved it to where it was right above the clip. Carefully, I rest it upon the clip. So far, so good.

While keeping my control on the clip and the book, my focus shifted to the giant textbook. This is where I failed before, I was quickly reminded as sweat started to bead up on my forehead. I looked down at my hands and could see they were shaking. I am so close. The text started to rise inches above the table. I started to hold my breath in anticipation. It lifted one inch, then another, before it finally was about a foot above the table. I couldn't lose it now.

Maintaining control and thinking that if this slammed down, not only would I have a ruined coffee table I cannot afford to replace, but also my favorite Nicole memento would be destroyed. Oh yeah, and I need this textbook for class too.

I allowed myself to take a deep breath, patience needed to be key here. That was my mistake last time, rushing through and losing control.

I started to lower the textbook until it was a hand's width away from the poetry book. I gripped my hands together to keep them from shaking and slowly continued to bring it down.

The textbook touched the poetry book, and I waited for the worst to happen. Just like before...

Wait. Did I actually do it? I was squinting my eyes, too afraid to see if I had failed.

I slowly opened them to spy a tower from smallest to largest; clip, then poetry book, then textbook, all perfectly balanced.

Huh. Maybe I can do some things right.

CHAPTER 4

SWEET DREAMS

The smell of cologne fills my nose and my heart starts to quicken. My palms start to sweat and I am suddenly aware of hundreds of butterflies fluttering around in my stomach.

I am eye to eye with the person I crushed on for years, who would always call me by my full name, would say cheesy jokes at the worst and best times, and who tried to kill me three months ago.

"Hey there, Isabel Grace. Funny seeing you here." His deep voice sent a shiver up my spine. Not sure if it was out of fear, or something else entirely.

"Parker? Wh-What are you doing here?" I stumbled out rushed words as I back away from his penetrating gaze that seemed to see straight through me.

He started singing to himself, okay is he losing it? Should I be running away? I can't seem to move, only stare at the man who used to consume my waking thoughts. I tried to listen to what he was singing under his breath. I swear I recognized the tune.

"Sweet dreams are made of this, who am I to disagree..." He smiled at me then as it dawned on me. I was dreaming.

"So, you're not real? This is just a dream."

"Oh Isabel Grace, I am very real. But yes, at this moment you are dreaming. But trust me, I am always around."

The haze of the dream was starting to clear up, and his features were becoming clearer.

I gasped when I saw what was on his face.

He was covered in scars, and I know for sure they weren't there the last time I saw him.

One crossed his right eyebrow, and was about an inch long. There was another the went down his left check, almost connecting his temple to his mouth. He pushed his hair off his head and I saw what else the dream haze was been hiding.

All over his hands, arms and I sure even more of his body was tons of tiny nicks. As if whoever did this was toying with him...as if he just had to sit and take it.

"Parker, wait, what happened?" I knew there wasn't before I would wake up and I needed to know what to do. How I could protect him.

"Don't worry Isabel Grace, I'll be seeing ya."

I wake up the next morning still smelling Parker's cologne. Woah. That seemed crazy real. I honestly have been trying to keep thoughts of Parker out of my head. But my dreams had a different idea last night I suppose.

What was the deal with the scars? Why would my subconscious give me that little freaky tidbit of visual? What am I supposed to do with that? I remember how I felt in the dream when I saw them, because I still feel it now...

I want to protect him. Why? Why on earth would I feel the need to protect someone who tried to kill me?

Despite the fact I am a good person, or at least I try to be, I still don't know if Parker would have actually gone through with the deed. I had to use pretty strong compulsion that day to will him to hang me. The note he left me said he would be around. But this dream was the first time I've seen him in months. Unless...No, I would known if he had been around.

I know his family was very hard core. I dreamed of his ancestor and know he was pretty terrible, so my imagination of his family wasn't much better. I can still feel his grubby hands on my face from my vision. Ugh. He referred to me as a "Devil Girl". I am very thankful his face no longer haunts my nightmares. If it came down to it, I would take Parker's face over his ancestor's ANY DAY.

I wonder how they reacted to him not killing me... when that was pretty much a years in the making mission to do so.

He said in his note that they weren't happy, does that mean they tortured him for it?

I can't let myself think too much on that, or else that's all I will be able to focus on.

Okay. Time to start my day and not think about crushes or ex crushes, whatever. I head to the bathroom to take care of my necessities, and then to the sink to brush my teeth.

It's not until I am about thirty seconds in when it hits me.

Last night I didn't dream of the nothing, instead I dreamed of Parker.

The first time in three freaking months I wasn't pulled into my subconscious, struggling to wake up. In fact, even with my Parker dream, this felt like the best sleep I have had in months. I felt rested, I felt ready to take on my day of school and magic lessons, I maybe even would say I felt...happy.

Happy isn't quite the right word, but I do know thinking of Parker feels right. Like the fact I haven't seen him in three months has made my life feel like it was lacking something.

I don't understand what exactly I feel about Parker, and how it all makes sense, but I do think he needs to be a part of my life. If my dreams mean something at least, and if I learned anything from my adventures from three months ago, that is that every dream and nightmare I have, happens for a reason.

Maybe I am supposed to save Parker. Even if he didn't save me then, maybe saving him could save me now.

CHAPTER 5

FRIENDS FIRST, SAVE THE DAY LATER

"Izzy!! I swear if you ignore another one of my calls again I am going to freaking lose it!" Yet another one of Nicole's friendly voicemails remind me I need to finally call her back.

I head to my favorites list and go ahead and FaceTime her. She may be just an apartment away, but its been over a week since she's actually seen my face.

Nicole loves FaceTiming too-every big news she's ever shared has been over FaceTime. She broke up with her boyfriend, immediately FaceTimed me to rehash the entire conversation. Got back together with said boyfriend, had me on FaceTime silently listening to the entire conversation so I could let her know later what was actually happening around all the gushy stuff. Got accepted into college, called me, then right after broke up with the same boyfriend so she would have a clean slate for college. Nicole is nothing if not consistent.

It rings once, and then I see Nicole's beautiful brown eyes looking back at me. Also a pair of dark blue worried eyes looking right at me.

"Elizabeth? Y'all hanging out? Ha, what, are you talking about me?" I nervously laugh.

"Yep" Nicole answers, and at the same time Liz says, "No!"

Um…What?

"Here's the deal, we were talking about you, but only because we are worried about you." Liz calmly states, her hand on Nic's arm as if she's holding her back.

"Guys, I am sorry I've been MIA. I've had some issues lately, but I think I am finally ready to figure it all out." Issues meaning I almost was killed, and now have been tempted to let myself succumb to nothing. You know, normal stuff.

'Ready to figure it all out' meaning Parker is the key to figuring out my issues. Find Parker, stop the nothing dreams. Simple enough.

"No, no, no, no, no. Hold the phone, Iz. You have been ignoring me I feel like for months. Even when you're here, you're not really here. You have been acting crazy ever since that Zachary guy came around. What is his deal? Is he making you this way?"

Liz comes in with a calm, "Iz, I know I haven't known you long, but I'm not stupid. I know something is up with you. I disagree though, I don't think this has to do with a boy. I think something is going on with you." Liz is too damn smart for her own good.

I guess in Nicole's head, that is exactly what happened. Zach appeared and all of sudden I start acting different. When honestly, stuff started happening before he came around. I wish I could tell her, heck, I wish I could tell both of them what really is different about me. I am a witch. I have powers and I am depressed? I know there's more to it than that, but that truly is the spark notes version.

I haven't let myself read minds lately, because of all the extra after school practice I have been doing. I already get headaches, I am trying not to use my powers when I don't have to. But the next time I see them, I may explore a bit. Maybe they could handle the truth. Is it fair of me to keep it from them? If I am able to talk about it, maybe that would help with the distancing I have been granting everyone around me.

"Trust me, I am working on it. I appreciate y'all. I truly have the best friends." Liz lit up a bit at that. We haven't officially been declared besties yet, but I feel really close to her. Nicole just nods knowingly, she's had that title for over fifteen years. She knows I couldn't live without her.

"Hey babe, just talk to us, okay? You don't have to handle everything on your own." Nicole said before they both said they loved me and their goodbyes. She nailed it right on the head.

That is truly my fatal flaw. Thinking I have to do everything by myself. I saw a counselor once, and didn't go back. Not because she wasn't right, but because she was too on the nose. I will never forget what she told me.

"How are you standing up straight right now?" The psychic counselor looked me straight in the eye and said, "You are carrying so much."

I cried for two hours after I left that appointment. I was too afraid to go back, even though its definitely crossed my mind lately. I felt seen. That was way before I knew about my powers too, that was just plain old Isabel.

Before we ended the call, I promised we would all meet up this week. No idea what I would say to them, but I would for sure try to open up. "Hi friends. So the reason I have been acting coo-coo for Cocoa Puffs is because...I am a witch."

How would that convo go? Would they try to admit me to a mental hospital? Would I blame them? No matter what, and no matter what I end up telling them exactly, they are my best friends. I need them.

Okay. So, a band aid has been put on the friends issue, now to handle some of my other issues.

Puff's meowing reminds me that I need to feed her before I handle anything else on my list. I dish out her food and try to get a handle on what to do next. I am for sure a list person- that helps my brain figure out what should take priority and what can handle the back burner for a bit. Here we go...

1. Online Classes- luckily I didn't have to leave my couch today for school, but I am the type that has to DO the assignment before it's DUE. It's the Due Date, not the DO date people!   UGHH I can't handle when people wait til the last minute. I may even try to do somethings without my powers, just to prove I still got it.

2. Magic Lessons with Zach- This time, without Valentina. Zach wants me to try being out and about in the world to see if that helps. I had told him about my successful attempt at stacking the items at home, so his new theory is that the Magic Shop may be messing with my head.

3. Figure out where Parker is and what to do about it. Don't tell Zach.

4. Lastly, and the one I am currently dreading is deal with Parker's family. They put out an order to kill me, that is not okay and most likely will happen again.

Before I embark on the trickier items on my list, I decide to get my school work over and done with. That way I won't have to worry about it while I am in full sleuth mode.

An hour and a half of my morning is dedicated to Anthropology and Statistics, and by 11:00, I finally pack away my laptop.

I was able to get through my homework the old fashioned way, no powers, just smarts. Cool, I still got it, guys. I was going to need all the help I could get power wise, so I needed to save myself just in time for my lunch and lesson with Zach.

We were going to start off at a hole in the wall taco shop and decide where to go from there for the lesson. Luckily the Taco shop was only about two blocks away from my apartment. I double check my weather app, see that it's sunny skies, and decide to walk the short distance.

I know better than to be on my phone while walking by myself outside. I needed all senses to be on alert. I am a twenty year old woman, I know the time I live in. So it wasn't too long into my walk that I started to feel a tingling all along my spine. The hairs on my arm started to stand straight up and I resist the urge to shiver.

Someone was watching me.

CHAPTER 6

SOMETHING IS ON THE MIND

I knew I couldn't stop walking, or else whoever was watching me would know that I knew they were there. I started to walk a little faster, trying to look out for Zach without seeming paranoid.

Three months ago, I wouldn't think anything of it, but after getting kidnapped and almost murdered, your perspective changes.

I drop down and pretend to tie my shoe, trying to catch a glimpse of my surroundings. I could see the taco stand was only on the next block. Up ahead of me was a sketchy alley I would have to walk right in front of to get to said Taco stand. Zach should be close, but do I risk it? I still have that feeling someone's watching me, but I see nothing out of the ordinary.

The alley is only about three feet across. I take a deep breath, and prepare myself to basically run across the alley. I zip on by and risk a quick glance in the depths of the small alleyway. Its completely dark but I swear I see a glow of hazel deep in the heart of the alley.

I quickly rush by, not wanting to think too hard on what or who that could be and basically sprint to meet Zach.

Earlier, I was starving and preplanning all of the glorious tacos I was going to order. Now, I have suddenly lost my appetite.

Freaking Zach Henley is smiling at me from across the street at the taco stand. Could he not have appeared five minutes ago?

"Hey Bel! Everything okay? You look like you've seen a ghost."

"Uh...maybe I did." I mumbled under my breath. Not wanting to worry him if there was nothing to worry about.

"What's up?" He asked, probably seeing through my act.

"Let's go, just get your tacos to-go. I'm not hungry anymore." I just started walking, knowing he would catch up. I know he was probably confused, thinking I was blowing him off. But I think he knows me well enough to know when I mean business.

He may not have been there five minutes ago, but if I truly needed him, Henley would be there. I know he wants to talk, figure out what's wrong with me, discuss what's next for us, but right now, I am all about the business. I need to figure my powers, then figure out what the absolute heck is going on. I also need to figure out what or who was just the alley. I have a pretty good idea...I just am praying I'm wrong.

To his credit, Henley is matching my power walk pace. All the while scarfing his birria taco down. I feel his worried glances, but I do not risk slowing down and meeting up with whatever was in the alley. Especially if its who I think it is... not with Henley here at least. Save that for another time, add it to the freaking giant list of problems that seems to be ever growing.

I finally start to slow down as we near my favorite book store. I feel the same calming vibes I get every time I enter. Zach steers me in, knowing its exactly what I need right now.

"Okay, whatever happened, You're safe. You're okay, Isabel." He grabbed me and pulled me in. Of course I immediately feel better. That's what Henley does to me, he makes me feel safe. I know that everything will work out with him. I also know I can't depend on him- he cannot save me every time I have a nightmare or see a shadow in an alley.

"You're right. I'm okay. Yes, I was freaked, but I really would like to focus on what we are here to do if that works for you." I shrugged off his comforting arms, knowing I would see the look of hurt flash across his face. That's what he can always count on I guess. I just hurt everyone. Him, Parker, Nicole, Elizabeth, heck even Puff is suffering because of me.

"Uh, Okay, if you're sure?" He reluctantly asked.

"Yes please, let's get on with it. I'm fine." I know he can see right through my fine. In fact, ANYONE who says they are "fine" is absolutely fucking lying to your face. They are not "fine", but they may not have the mental capacity to accept that they are not "fine". I am fine though, that rule just applies to everyone else. Well...I need to be fine, so I will be.

"Alright, well then let's get started," Zach Henley looked at me then, willing me to talk to him, help me share my worries, know that he will always be here for me. I could practically feel his support radiating towards me.

"I want to work on your mind reading. I feel like that's the one you put off the most, and it's actually the one that saved your life." What he is referring to wasn't really my mind reading. Though I was seeing all the ways Parker was cooking up to kill me three months ago. He had a very vivid imagination, so it was pretty terrifying. Zach was actually talking about my mind influencing, how I influenced Parker to put me on the rope, allowing myself to be hung. Which ultimately resulted in me saving myself, or almost saving myself...Zach had to swoop in and carry me at the last second.

I know that the mind reading and influencing was vital that night, but I disagree. I think my dreams saved me, which is why I will not miss a warning from them ever again. I hate that I have not had three months worth of dreams. What am I missing that I could be learning? My past self or ancestor whoever she was, seemed to think I had much more ahead of me. Was she the one who sent me the dream about Parker?

Clearing my head, I listened to find out what Zach wanted me to do for my mission of the day.

"See that couple over there?" I look over in the direction he's referring to. Seated over next to the bookstore coffee stand, is a couple who seem heated in hushed conversation. The bookstore truly is the best. Who needs television when you have drama right in front of you?

"You may not be able to hear what they're saying, but tell me what they're thinking." He knows I have only read people's minds of those I care about. To be honest, I try to not even do that. It feels like a breach of privacy, especially if they don't know I can do it. Like yes, I know all of your deep, dark secrets, and Hell no, I am not telling you mine. It just doesn't seem fair.

"Um, Okay. I'll try."

"You got this, Bel." He smiles at me, and honestly I know 'I got this.' That's the confidence his smile gives me; he believes I can truly do anything, so why should I stand in my own way?

I take a deep breath, my calming techniques on standby if I need them. I focus on the couple. The girl seems to be about late twenties and the male in his early thirties. Both attractive, the kind of couple who seems like they are the "it" couple, but my goal is to find what is behind those million dollar smiles.

The tall olive skinned, brunette looks up at the blonde hair, blue eyed, cutie expectantly. Before I even attempt to read her mind, I know Mr. Perfect is in trouble.

Ronnie (that's Mr. Perfect's name) needs to get his shit together. Cal has been waiting and waiting, and is sick and tired of everyone and their mom, hers included, asking when he is proposing. They have been dating for two years for chrissakes! Angelina (Cal's best frenemy) just got engaged and her and her boyfriend only dated for five months?! What the actual fuck?!

I was fighting the urge to slap Zach...reading Cal's mind put me right in her emotions. Not even sure why I had a reason to be mad at Zach but I definitely was feeling some anger towards him.

"Take it easy, Iz, take all the time you need, sometimes these things take a while."

"What made you the expert in MY powers, Zachary?" I ask him accusingly. In my right mind, I know he didn't do anything to deserve this, but I am not in my my mind, I am still in Cal's.

"Well, I uh, just mean that when you, I mean people try out their powers it can be overwhelming."

"Why do you always do that? Assume you know everything about me? You know NOTHING Zachary Henley. And who the fuck are you? You just appear one day and now you want to be a huge part of my life? Relationships are meant to be reciprocated! You are asking me to give, even when I have nothing TO give, and you haven't given me anything in return!"

Whoa, I blew up. Cal brought out some deep feelings. Poor Zach looked like Puff after a forced bath. Shriveled and puny. To be fair, Zach had been there for me. I just needed so much more. I think that's why I haven't let myself open up to him and dive in to a relationship. I honestly barely know him. He acts like we've known each other for years, but honestly, its been three months.

I cringe as the couple I was just spying on is now openly staring at me have a meltdown.

Poor guy. She seems nuts. Cool cool cool. They are thinking that about me. I love that for my self esteem.

"Yeah...I got to go Zach. I clearly am too unhinged to be doing this right now. " I leave him and he seems to still be in shock over my explosion.

Should I have taken all my anger out on him? Should I have let Cal's emotions be a gateway drug to my burst? Was I telling the truth and did those words need to be said to him?

No, no, and yes.

CHAPTER 7

MIC DROP

The hay prickles my back as I roll over. I can't seem to get comfortable. Wait a minute…Hay?

I realize I am not in my plush Temper-Pedic dupe, but I am in fact laying on a hay stuffed mattress. A single hay currently poking me in the butt. I groan and shift, and as I do I notice the man sleeping next to me.

I am trying not to freak out as there is an actual MAN in bed with me. If you can call this torture device a bed. I can't freak out, I can't freak out. If I do, he will wake up and instead of dealing with a sleeping man in my bed, I will be dealing with an awake man! Take a breath Iz, what's going on?

I finally start to notice something else off. I am not in my second floor apartment, but I am in what looks to be a small cabin. There is no AC, there is no television in the corner, there is not laptop putting off a small greenish glow as it charges on my nightstand. There's not even a nightstand to be seen. I sneak out of the hay bed, making sure not to wake my sleeping friend. I need light to see more. I see light creeping under the wooden door frame. It must almost be sunrise.

I sneak out, and realize we are definitely not in Kansas anymore. I am wearing a night gown that has to be from another century. I am also wearing what I can only think of as a night cap, tied neatly under my chin. Okay…should I start freaking out now?

"Good Morrow Isabel. " My bedmate is at the door, smiling at me.

"Good Morrow Zachariah." The person who was me in the dream answered. What the hell?

Then its as if someone clicked the "next" button on the remote to my life. I see the same man, a hundred different ways, in what seems to be a hundred different times.

"Morning, Izzie." Says the man, wearing a trench coat and a fedora.

Flash!

"Morning Glory!" Smiled the man, now sporting a handsome leather jacket and jeans, his normally short hair now long and slicked back.

Flash!

"Sup." A grunge rocker man now stood before me.

The flashes started to speed up, where I couldn't tell what was happening or more importantly, when was happening.

But I knew one thing for sure. Zachary Henley was the man in every single flash.

I wake up, feeling confused, annoyed, and possibly betrayed. I just had the craziest dream.

If it was true, it could mean I have known Zach a VERY long time. I know I saw him in my dreams before, but nothing like this. He appeared so many times, and he was the same ole Zach. Even if he was dressed a hundred different ways, it was still him. I know that in my very core.

I also have the feeling I was still me... I was still Isabel Grace. Not some distant relative, but me, in a different time...this is some multiverse level shit here. I don't think my brain can handle this. I was just focused on going day by day and now I have to look back on hundreds of possible Isabels?

Distraction. That's what I need. Something to take my mind off whatever is going on. Hmmm my lesson did get cancelled abruptly, I guess I could practice some powers?

I spy Puff relaxing in her sunshine corner. She lays by the balcony sliding door on her very own pillow. Eyes closed, completely basking in the sun. It's her favorite spot to be 90% of the time. The other ten is when she's receiving pets from me. That's me being generous assuming she even cares to give my pets ten percent.

I sit on the couch, all the while keeping my gaze on my little white poof ball. I imagine scratching her behind her velvet ears, knowing that's her favorite spot. I see in my mind's eye rotating my hand, switching from left ear, to right. I know my mental pets are indeed working, as Puff's increasingly loud purr is intensifying with each moment.

I decide to test myself even further. I imagine picking Puff up from underneath her armpits of her two front paws, Lion King style. This isn't her favorite way to be picked up, but it's definitely mine.

I watch in awe as Puff floats up from her pillow and rises in the air, as if Casper himself is picking her up. I am so focused on Puff floating, that I don't hear my front door being opened. I don't notice anything actually, purely focused on keeping her afloat, until I hear Nicole start screaming.

The next thing I know, Puff has fallen on her pillow and screeches at me, before running off to sanctuary under my bed. Luckily the rumors are true, cats always land on their feet.

I am scared to even turn around. I know Nicole is still standing in the doorway. But I have been avoiding this conversation for months now. Maybe she will just assume Puff is the one with powers? Like some sort of Super Kitty? It could happen, that's not what happened, but hey, anything is possible, right?

"Whew." I let out a giant exhale. I know this conversation is about to go down, and I don't know if I am ready for it.

"What the actual fuck is happening, Isabel?" That is one of the things I love about Nicole, she doesn't beat around the bush. Even in elementary school, she was the one who would march right up to the boy she liked, and proceed to chase him around the playground. She's never been scared of anything, protecting me and has always been there for me.

Once when we were older, the summer after high school, she was vacationing with her family about three hours away from our hometown. My high school boyfriend dumped me, and I was heartbroken. My naive self believed we would settle down and get married, and have the family I never really did. Looking back, I should have expected it. But at the time, it totally broke me. Nicole ditched her family, rode three different busses, and one train and made it back to me that same night. I didn't ask her to, she just came. That's the thing with Nicole, you never had to ask, and she would always come anyways. I think that's the biggest thing that's been holding me back. What if this is it? What if this is the thing that makes her leave?

"Nic, I need you to calm down for a second." I could hear her thoughts running around in circles, and I was too mentally exhausted to try and shut them out.

That was the wrong thing to say apparently.

"I need to calm down? I just witnessed your cat floating five feet above the ground, and I'm the one who needs to calm down? "

"I know, I'm sorry, I just…I don't really know what to say here."

"There's nothing to say, except the truth."

I wait, knowing what question was next. I wasn't afraid to say it, I had practiced saying it in my head for the past three months. I was afraid of what she would say.

"Isabel Grace. You need to be honest for once. You have been lying to me and I have known you your whole life. I am essentially the only family you have." I know its coming. I take another deep breath, hoping my calming techniques could save me once again. But there's no senses trick to save me now.

"Do you have powers?" She looks at me, with such focus, I do not dare look away.

"Yes, I am a witch."

CHAPTER 8

THEY ALL LEAVE

I wait for the implosion. I just told my best friend I was a witch. I know I could read her mind, but honestly I am terrified of what she is thinking.

"Say something, please. Just don't say I'm crazy. I mean I am, but not in the way you're thinking." My ramble begins. "Just the depressed, anxious, overthinking kind of way. This power stuff, is real." I am afraid to even look at Nicole. So I just continue my incoherent babble. " I know I should have told you, I just didn't want to lose you. You're right, you are the only family I have. If I lost you, I would have no one." I finally risk a glance at Nicole.

She has this distant look in her eye. She feels like she doesn't even know me anymore.

"That's not true! You know me better than anyone!" I watch her mouth drop. Shit. That was in her head. I read her mind without even realizing.

"Did. You. Just. Read. My. Mind." Each word comes out like its own sentence, with such force behind each quite word. She finally looks at me, and I see it. I see how she feels I have betrayed her.

"Uh. Yes. But does it help if I didn't mean to? I have only been doing this a couple of months, and I don't have a lot of control yet, especially when emotions are running high..." I know I am babbling again. I just can't stand the way she's looking at me. It's like I am a stranger to her.

"I can explain. Let's sit, you can make us some tea, and I can finally tell you everything." I beg, hoping she would listen , would give me a chance.

"Isabel, I cannot deal with this, with you, right now. I...I gotta go." She turns and without a second look over her shoulder. My best friend walks out my door, possibly walks out of my life.

I gasp as the door slams. More air that I hiccup in and in, my heart tightens, yet I can't let the air go. I start hyperventilating as the tears fall. I feel my heart pounding in my chest. Thump thump...thump thump... thump Thump thump thump. It just gets quicker and quicker, until I hear nothing but thump thump thump.

I feel my body start to shake as it hits me. The one person who I knew in my heart would never leave, just left out the door. I see Puff run over to me just as everything goes black.

I wake up in a man's arms. I immediately freak out, thinking I am dreaming again of my past life or whatever.

"Sup, Bel. How's it hanging?" What. I know that cocky attitude.

"Parker, what are you doing here?"

"You tell me babe, this is your dream." I look around, suddenly realizing what he said was true. I must have passed out from my panic attack. Great. Puff probably was losing it. I would be covered in kitty kisses when I woke up. I look at Parker and see he is still covered in scars.

"What happened to you?" I run my had across his cheek, where the worst one was. He leans into my hand and closes his eyes.

"It was worth it. You're okay." His eyes suddenly snap open. "Wait, Bel, I have to focus. I need to tell you something. I'm here to warn..."

"Shh, its okay. I realized from the last dream that I need to find you. I know you need saving. Just give me a little more time." I reassure him.

"That's not it...They're coming! You need to stay far away from me. Just stay with Henley, he's safe." He rushed through the words, barely making sense. He looks around, as if others are watching in the shadows.

"There's no time, I'm sorry, I need to say more. There's just no-" He gets cut off as I feel water splash my face.

"Isabel! Wake up! Are you okay?" The other man of my dreams is currently standing over me, with a once full bottle of water. Oh yeah, and I am freaking drenched.

"Why am I covered in water, Zach?" I start to get up and reach to grab the towel in his other hand.

"Puff found me. She was freaking out, and I walk in and see you on the ground. And uh.. I started freaking out. I'm sorry Iz. " He sheepishly answered, avoiding eye contact.

"Unless you have more water ready to throw, can I have one to actually drink?"

"Uh, sure." Zach opens my fridge and grabs one water, handing it to me as I dry myself off. "So, care to explain the whole passed out on the floor thing?"

"Nicole knows. It was a whole thing." I stand up, avoiding his helping hand. I walk around him to settle back on the couch. "But I can't think about that right now, but there is something we need to talk about."

"I have been so ready to talk, Iz. I can't stand not being with you all of the time. You make the world make sense. I know you're dealing with a lot, but we are stronger when we're together." He sounds so convincing, I hope he has no idea what I am about bring up.

"Zach. Have we met before? Like many, many, times?"

He was ready for a lot, but he wasn't ready for that.

"Uh, yes. Um...How did you find out?" He looked down and bit his lip.

"WHAT. THAT'S YOUR QUESTION! HOW DID I FIND OUT?!" I blow up at the man who I apparently have known many years, even though to my memory, only three months. "WHAT THE FUCK ARE WE?"

"We're soulmates, Isabel." He smiles at me, a glow in his eyes. "We have lived many lives, but each time we find each other. We are meant to be, together, forever." He tries to take my hand, I shake it off. I need to think clearly for this conversation.

"How come you remember? I just met you, literally three months ago..."

"Iz, we've known each other for almost five hundred years." My heart stops. Five. Hundred. Years. What?! " I know this is a lot, but trust me, I am here for you, just like I always have been here for you." He thinks he's saying all the right things, but he is not. "You see, I remember everything. My lives all thread into this one. I am the same Zachariah Henley that I once was. You, are a little different each life, but this one is the most different I would say. You never know me, but you still love me in every life." He reaches for my hand again, I stand up.

I cannot be here. I cannot take another second of this. Henley is just trying to comfort me with his understanding eyes, but he doesn't get it. How can I just accept this fate? Sure, with time, I may love Henley, but how do I know now if I loved him because I was supposed to, or because I truly loved him? How could he be okay with that? I need to make the choice of who I love on my own terms, not his and definitely not freaking destiny.

"You need to leave. I need to be by myself. You tell me three months ago I am a witch, and now there's such thing as soulmates? This is too much." I walk him towards my door.

"Wait, Iz, we really should be together while we figure this out." He starts, but that is the exact opposite of what I want.

"Zachary Henley. You leave right now. I can't be around you, not now, possibly ever."

I watched the once bright light leave his eyes. He slowly backed away from the door frame. I waited til he was clear, then I slammed it in his face.

CHAPTER 9

THE WORST IS YET TO COME

A part of me wants to feel bad for him. This life is all he knows. We meet, we fall in love, then its happily ever after, again and again. From what it sounds like, he is just constantly waiting for me every single life. Henley made it sound like such a gift to be soulmates, but hearing it aloud made it sound like a curse, especially for him.

I at least have lived a life separate from him. His whole existence revolves around me. UGHHHH. I hate that! I hate that for me, I hate that for him! Why does destiny get to decide our choice for us? You are taught every fairy tale that one day you grow up, you fall in love, and have a happily ever after. What if I want to be the one who makes that choice? I want to live my own freaking happily ever after- not one decided for me.

He doesn't understand. He only knows this life, and doesn't know it could be better. What if there's another true love waiting for him, that is so much better than me, but he is refusing to give the option even a chance?

Maybe Henley and me are soulmates, I do really care about him, and he does make everything wrong in the world feel right. But I want to be the one to decide that, not some unknown entity that decided this hundreds of years ago. Five hundred years of the same story. Why haven't the powers that be gotten sick of the same ole love story already? I just heard it, and I am already looking for a loophole.

Like I said, a part of me feels bad, but the larger part of me, is mad as hell. Why did he keep this monumental thing from me? How can we supposedly spend our lives (Note the plural) together, if he lies half the time? I am HUGE on honesty. I would rather be heart broken and know the truth, than have my life sugarcoated in lies and half truths.

The more I think about it, the more mad I get. I am pacing my small apartment, only worrying Puff more with each lap. It's not until the sun starts to go down that I notice my endless pacing and worrying has resulted in hours going by. I was stuck in my own head for hours, with only Puff's random meows to keep me in reality.

I need to get out of here. Other wise another two hours will pass by with me stuck in my own thoughts. Whenever I feel trapped and straddled with a problem, I go into research mode. So that's what I decide to do- head to the library. So multiple lives? I have absolutely no idea what that means. Why does Zach remember his lives every time, and my memory starts over each life? I make a plan to research every past me- and see if anything comes up.

I give Puff a quick pet, lay out her food, not knowing how long this study sesh will go. If I get rolling, it could be hours. But I also could be back in twenty minutes. Only the library knows the answers...

Walking out the door, ready to take the short walk to the city library, there's one thing I want to do. Only one person who is there every time I need someone. Who even though they are PISSED at me, I still want to talk to them.

I press Nicole's number on speed dial, number one in my phone and in my life, no matter that she may not ever forgive me for lying to her. How am I any better that Zach? I feel my eyes well up as I hear the phone ring.

I want to tell her everything. This whole time, I truly think I have been struggling because I wasn't able to tell my person everything. I can't deal with it without Nicole being there with me. She would let me pull myself out of the hole of darkness, but she would be there next to me, every step of the way. She would make me pull myself up, but then she would have a tea waiting. She lets me fight my battles, but she is cheering me on the whole time. She knows I have to win those battles on my own, so she lets me. But she also knows I don't like being alone, no matter how much of a loner I am. She's my person. I need her.

By the sixth ring, I am about to hang up, when her voice message starts.

"Hey, this is Nicole, if you need me- Freaking text me you weirdo. Who calls anymore? Stalker. Iz- if this is you- you call me anytime. Anything for you weirdo." BEEP. I brush the fallen tear form my cheek as I stop in my tracks on the streets.

"Nic, I love you. I need to talk to you. Here's the deal, you may not want me in your life and that's too bad. You're stuck with me. You can't get rid of me. You are my family, and yes I lied. It honestly was because of this- I was terrified of losing you. You are the best thing in my life. I am having all this boy drama- like Parker is a witch hunter who disappeared but could be haunting me; Zach is my soulmate and apparently we've been together for five hundred years. I know! I also have been struggling with all of this mentally and each day has been a battle, I know I am saying this all to a machine, but I LOVE YOU.   I just can't handle all of this without you. I am running to the library for research mode but please call—"

I can't finish my long message, not because I overran the time limit, but because I am suddenly shrouded in darkness. A smelly cloth is shoved aggressively in my mouth as I am grabbed from behind. Everything goes black, I fall to the concrete, hoping someone will catch me.

CHAPTER 10

ALONE?

I wake up, still nothing but darkness, but now I am laying down with hay poking my back. Ugh. Is this another dream? I am deciding now- I hate hay.

Dream or no dream, I need to figure out what is happening. I struggle to move, only to find I am bound. My hands are tied behind my back and my ankles are hog tied together. I have some sort of bag over my head. They literally tossed me in some barn like a bag of flour. Now to figure out, who is they?

Was this Parker? He kidnapped me before, would he do it again? He may be desperate to get in his family's good graces. When I read his mind, they seemed hard core. I also met their descendent, and I can see where they get it from.

Wait. It can't be. Was that what Parker was warning me about? Because of everything with Zach, I haven't had time to process my dream with Parker. I thought he was asking me to save him, but maybe he was trying to save me?

My sense of hearing is more sensitive since I can't see anything. So ordinarily I may not have picked up on the footsteps coming from a nearby hallway, but right now I could hear every step. A sense of dread settled over me. The footsteps are so close, now I can hear the heavy breathing. I stay still, like a possum playing dead. If I don't move, maybe they will move on.

My captor snatches the bag off my head, not falling for my ploy. He kicks me sharply in the ribs, and pulls me up to a sitting position by my ponytail. I can't help but yell, no matter how much I don't want to give him the satisfaction of knowing he hurt me.

"Hey Bitch. I mean Witch." Oooo. I hate this guy already. Still gripping my ponytail, he looks me right in the eye, inches away from my face. I feel his breath seeping in my pores. He definitely looks related to Parker, but where Parker is all smiles, this man is evil incarnate. I am almost afraid to look into his thoughts, knowing what darkness awaits. But I know if I have any chance of getting out this, I need to know everything I can, including who exactly is this sick son of a bitch.

I allow myself inside his mind, feeling disgusting, like I am trespassing in a serial killer's apartment. Which honestly, he may be one.

I learn his name is Hyde Hunting. Yes, the Jekyll and Hyde reference is not lost to me. He is Parker's older brother, and in his mind- the pride and joy of the family. Which pretty much means he is my worst nightmare. I start to dive deeper, and I see a memory from just a few months ago. A face I know, getting torn to shreds. Parker. He was tortured by his own family. All because of me. I start to look more, trying to find out what he did and did not tell them. But I am quickly brought back to reality as I am slammed into the floor once again.

"Hey! Bitch! I am talking to you! I heard a lot about you, but I didn't peg you for rude! I guess you are a spawn of the devil. Shouldn't be surprised." Oh here we go again. Devil spawn. This family is NUTS. How Parker managed at least some sanity growing up with these loons is amazing. He was meant to be my enemy, and yet, he went against the odds. Huh. Focus. I am in very dangerous territory right now.

"How can I hear anything when you slam my face into the ground?" I wait on the ground for his wrath, as he inches closer to me. Whispering right in my ear, tingles and shivers go up my spine.

"Watch your mouth, witch. You got a world of pain coming your way, so you want me to be your friend. I can make it hurt real good." His whispers slide down my skin like a eel. I swallow, and try to stay still, even though I want to be as far away from him as possible. "My family has plans for you, Isabel." Hearing my name come from his mouth does it, releases the small hold of control I had- I immediately vomit. Luckily, he is grossed out.

"Disgusting wench." He slams the door, leaving me cheek first in my own vomit. I roll to the other side, knowing my hair is now covered. At least my sensitive stomach came in clutch. But I know this is only a temporary fix. I have to get out of here if I plan to survive. I know he will be back.

PARKER'S VIEW

The worst has happened. She's gone. I tried to watch her. But every time I watched her, they watched me. It's all my fault. I tried to stay away. The magic store was close- she almost caught me. I was going to say goodbye. Keeping her safe was priority and I decided then and there the best thing to do was leave.

I would be broken, but she would be safe. I was all set to leave when I noticed my family tailing her. That day in the alley, they were lurking, ready to snatch. If I would have been five seconds later, they would have grabbed her. Instead, we were hidden in the shadows, luckily this time I had the upper hand. That is not always the case.

I brush a hand across my pink scar. I am starting to get used to it after three months of staring it in the mirror everyday. I could have walked away unscathed if I would have gave everything away, all her secrets. But I didn't, and I failed my task, thus was punished and banished. I am scum now, but at least she is safe, or she was.

I decided to stick around after the alley, Isabel was constantly in my thoughts and even my dreams, which I swear were real. I tried to warn her, but she was adamant about saving me?! When her life was in danger, she was worried about me? How selfless is that? How could she be a 'devil spawn' when she only thinks of others? She is pure, and good, and my family is the evil one.

But I really failed this time. She's gone. I lost eyes on her, thinking she was still in her apartment with Henley. But, I lost her. Now she's gone.

So, here I am, outside of my sworn enemy's apartment. Because two men can suck it up and get over a centuries long rivalry to save the woman they both love. Oops. Haven't admitted that before to myself. Cool. Cool. I'm in love. Cool. She's a witch. She's currently god knows where with my witch murdering family. Cool. Cool. Fuck it.

Knock. Knock.

"What do you want Hunter?"

"You know its Hunting, and you also know, I'm retired. Isabel is in trouble. We have to save her." A flurry of emotions run across his face- sadness, disbelief, and finally, resolve.

"Let's get our girl." Say what you want about Zach Henley, but he will move heaven and earth for Isabel. Well, get in line pal.

We sit on his outdoor porch and make a plan. I don't think he trusts me in his apartment. I don't blame him. I wouldn't trust me either.

I have a pretty good idea where they have her. The family has a barn about twenty miles outside of town. Makes them feel like it's the good old days- hay beds, churning your own butter, murder on your own terms, all the fixings. I hate it there. I have nightmares of what's been done on that property, what could be happening to Bels right now.

I shake it off- focus man. You will save her, you have to save her.

We start our journey, in my truck, against his will.

"So, this is it right?" He starts, and in prepare for the worst, but focus on the road ahead. "This is where she was when you drugged her." He's right. I had a car air freshener that made her pass out. It's actually one for the nicer ways to make someone pass out, it seems fucked up, but I was trying to make it better for her.

"Yes. Any more questions, or can we focus on trying to save her and get her past my family? Oh, and not die ourselves?"

"You really think they would kill you? Their family?"

"Yes- never stopped them before." That shut him up.
Thank god. I have nightmares about Bel and I see all the
things that could have happened. I hate myself and I don't
need him reminding me.

The rest of the drive is silent. We went over the plan
enough- park a mile out, split up, and find points of
weakness. Come back and figure out the best way to get her
out. Together.

Seems pretty solid. I feel as confident as possible, until we
pull up to our designated spot and see my brother standing in
the middle of the road. Knives in both hands. His weapon of
choice. Wicked smile filling up his face as he looks at us.
Shit.

"Hey, Bitch. Look who I found."

Ew. I guess I really did pass out in my own throw up from
earlier today. This is a new low for me. Hyde had a few
visits with me today, I guess I lost track. I roll over, thinking
this can't get much worse. Boy, I am dead wrong.

Parker and Zach are walking in- Hyde has a knife next to both of their throats.

What?! Why are they here? Hold on. Are they saving me? Two sworn enemies? The witch hunter and the witch.

I start cracking up. This is ridiculous. Tears come to my eyes, I am laughing so hard. This just seems like a Stan Lee comic or something.

An older version of Hyde and Parker strides in. A man in his fifties, that probably could be handsome if life hadn't hardened him against everything that is good in the world.

He slaps me across the face and pulls me up to standing- which is very difficult with your hands and ankles tied. What is this family's deal with casually slapping everyone? What happened to just talking?

So, this is their dad. Great.

Mr. Hunting grips me by the shoulder, nails digging in.

"Shut up witch. Hyde, whatcha got for me? I see the trash got washed up." He smirks over at Parker. Shit, shit, shit. Why did he come here? He is gonna get killed. "Guess we didn't hit you hard enough last time if you can still walk." What the hell were they thinking?

"Hey Dad. Yeah, just wanted to come down for the weekly abuse. It's like my vitamin C or something- ha." There's that cocky attitude. He always acts like he is the biggest man on campus, but I can see his hands shaking. I look over at Henley in disbelief. He only is looking at me. His eyes are full of worry, not for himself, but for me. I wonder what I must look like. Hyde definitely has had some fun with me, but after that first time, I just went to my void. It only seemed to make him go harder. The more he hit me, the deeper I went in. I was safe. It wasn't until he finally swore and gave up, I would pull myself out.

I look back to just a week ago- when it was so hard to wake up each morning. The void was a curse, just like my dreams used to always be. Now it's become a gift, just like my dreams did. The void is a safe space for my mind, even when my body is being throttled. They can't break me, because my mind is where my true power lies. As long as I have that- I can survive. The body can heal, the mind can't always come back. So I have been using the one power that's available to me right now, my void inside my mind. The bad thing is, it can't do jack to protect the two most important men in my life.

I look around. We are in a ratty barn, with a wall full of farming tools that I can only imagine double as torture materials. The rusty pitchfork is screaming murder and tetanus shot. Henley and Parker currently are trapped with knives jammed in their throat. One wrong move, and they are a breath away from a carotid artery and bleeding out on the dirty floor. That's not even including me. If I jump to save them, Mr. Hunting will do all the things floating in his brain to me.

He wants to throttle me, pick me up by the neck and show me how his son of a bitch son was supposed to do his job. He was going to make his ancestors proud. I was the one who kept getting away, even if I died, I kept coming back like a plague. He wanted to cure the world of me, once and for all. If hanging didn't work, he had this book that should work...Oh God. I got to get out of this psychopath's head.

We are so screwed.

I am ready to give up, when I hear an engine in the distance, getting closer. Mr. Hunting and Hyde look at each other quizzically.

Suddenly, we all are forced to dive out of the way as Parker's giant truck comes crashing into the barn.

On the floor, I start crawling away towards the boys, and away from Old man Hunting. Luckily- the mystery crash helped with my ropes, or maybe I finally was able to loosen them with my powers. I am DONE asking questions when good things come my way. Like with two boys looking pitiful on the floor- I have two great guys, that would do anything for me. I need to stop thinking that's a problem and just enjoy their friendship. They risked their lives to save me, that is HUGE.

I grab them and start pulling them up, one in each hand, definitely using my powers to help me out. They are definitely heavier than a freaking rock. They look confused and shaken up, since they got a lot of the hit from the debris flying. I look over and Hyde is knocked out cold; he's got planks of wood covering his body, criss crossing and blocking my view of his legs. That's one less problem to deal with.

We start running, or as close to running as our broken bodies can handle to the truck; ready to meet our mysterious savior. We look as the window to the driver's seat rolls down, and we are all shocked when we see who it is.

"Hey losers, need a ride?" Nicole cocks a grin and unlocks the doors.

CHAPTER 11

THE GANG IS BACK

We don't stop and ask questions, we just quickly scramble and get in the truck. We speed up and get the hell of dodge. All of us are just staring at Nicole. She doesn't seem to get the hint.

She waits until we are about ten minutes away from the torture barn and looks around, "What is everyone staring at?"

"Um, thank you for saving us..." Henley starts. "But uh I think we're all wondering..."

"No offense, babe, but I think we are just wondering how the hell you just saved us." There goes Parker, going straight to the point, while Henley was trying to be polite.

"Since I just saved you all...and you look very beat up right now, I will excuse the attitude, Mr. Witch Hunter." Parker's eyes got big, I forgot I told her everything on the word vomit voicemail.

"So, even though me and witch bestie aren't on the best of terms, I actually listened to her voicemail. She told me everything, and I was halfway through listening to her long message, when I decided I needed to see her in person." She looked at me, and I felt tears come to my eyes. She still loved me. Nicole cleared her throat, going back to her story, and keeping her eyes on the road.

"I was almost to the apartment, when I noticed she got cut off. When my Bel girl is on a rant, there's no stopping her. I knew something was wrong." Wow. I guess she really knows me, or I am just predictable. Ha.

Nicole continues, "I checked everywhere, Parker's place, Zach's place, the library, and when I couldn't find you, my mind went to the worst. I just had this horrible feeling you were not okay. I looked up properties owned by the Huntings and it wasn't too hard to deduce you were probably trapped at that murder barn." Glad I am not the only person who thinks so! "I followed my gut, and it led me right to your truck, Parker. I saw the keys were dropped on the ground and figured you both needed rescuing too! You're welcome, by the way." She looked pointedly at their sorry butts in the back seat.

"Thanks". "Yeah, ditto." Both boys mumbled in the back, a little embarrassed their rescue was taken from them.

"Anyways, I followed the road, and still my gut just said 'go faster!', so I did! I rammed your truck into murder barn and I am so glad I did. Insurance probably covers murder evading, right?"

She reached over and grabbed my hand. She has a variety of teas for me to choose from as soon as we lose these boys and get to her apartment. She just loves me so much, no matter what I am.

"I love you too, Nic." I squeeze her hand. She jumps slightly, still not used to my mind reading. Then, she squeezes it right back.

We got a long road ahead, including hospital check ups for the three of us, lots of tea talks, and god knows we are all due for a major come-to-Jesus meeting with ALL of us. But for now, I am here with my best friend, in a truck full of people I care about, and who care about me, ready for another day.

EPILOGUE

He would have revenge. He had never felt so humiliated.

His son is in the hospital, the coward. Few planks of wood were enough to knock him out. He never was man enough for this family. Parker was the one who should have been on the right side of the fight. He was groomed to take over it all, then the little shit fell in love with scum. Rookie mistake.

His first kill was quick, but he will never forget it. He never forgets any of them. But this one, now is personal. She escaped, turned his son against him, and has robbed every family member before him of their true kill. It definitely won't be quick.

She is no ordinary witch, so no ordinary kill will do for her, she needs something special. He will make his forefathers proud. He will do what they could never do, and he will kill her line once and for all. Her existence will be extinct.

He would do whatever possible, even if it went against the very core of everything he stood for. He was ready.

The bell rang as he walked through the door of the magic shop. There were shriveled animal parts and vials of God knows what on the rows of the shelves. He walked on, he was looking for something in particular. He walked right up to the counter, to a bohemian dressed shopkeeper.

"Greetings, sir." He suppressed a shiver as the vile creature spoke to him. "How can I help you?" She smiled at him, not knowing who he was.

"I'm looking for a book," he said with a smile.

END OF BOOK 2.

PROLOGUE

It started as the others had; flames everywhere, I was held down and restricted from any movement or any way out. I was trapped- and once again, I had a miserable-looking, grimy man in front of me.

"Has thou had enough?" He sneered at me, grabbing my chin and turning it to face him. His familiar face has haunted me my entire life- eyes that seemed to be soulless, scruff adorning his cheeks, and a familiarity to someone I care about I always try to forget.

One thing I have learned since the start of these, I can fight back.

I spit in his face, dirt running down his cheek, and waited for the strike to hit as he swung back his hand. I flinch, even though I know it's not real.

He freezes midair. His hand six inches away from my face. I look around and try to see beyond the flames and angry villagers surrounding us.

Walking through the flames is my knight in shining armor, he is coming to save the day. I know he will keep me safe, and now that he is here, everything is going to be okay. Butterflies start in my stomach, and even though I am surrounded by terror, I still get excited as he approaches.

I just can't see his face.

CHAPTER 1

HELLO, AGAIN

I wake up, immediately glaring a hole in my ceiling. I turn over towards my bedside table and check my phone-3 am. Cool. Who needs sleep anyway? I swear I survive most of my life on two to three hours a night. Not always consecutively.

I feel for new moms out there- I am but a simple college student, aspiring witch, who still cannot control her dreams even after a year of knowing she is a witch. But at least they get a cute baby with their lack of sleep...all I get is tortuous nightmares that may or may not have actually happened to me in a past life, and then a mysterious savior. The question used to be, why did I get haunted by these dreams? I now know the answer.

I am a witch.

My dreams were a part of my powers showing me more of who I am and who I could become. Sometimes they would show me a premonition of what is to come, other times they have actually shown me snippets of my past lives.

Yeah. Turns out my soul is hundreds of years old, give or take a few decades. That was a fun surprise. When the biggest news of my sophomore year of college wasn't you're a witch, but instead- you are a reincarnated soul, 'twas a bit of a shocker to say the least.

But actually, the biggest, gnawing question I currently have after waking up from my dream- Who the hell was my knight?

I would assume it's Zachary Henley-Zach or Henley for short depending on what mood I am currently in. He's supposed to be my soulmate or whatever. Most of my dreams of my past lives, he is a constant. We shared every single life together. He remembers them all, while I only get the flashes from my dreams. He has loved me his entire existence, while I am still so new to the world of witchery around me. I know I feel safe in his arms, and I feel like the world can be right, as long as we are together. If the knight who saved me was in fact Henley, that might mean this isn't a dream, but a memory.

But, there is someone else the knight could be.

Someone who also has moved heaven and earth to save me, even at the risk of his own life. He only has just the one-and he gambled it for me. Parker Hunting.

Mind you- he also kidnapped me, with the full intention of killing me. It was part of his family legacy- they are a family of witch hunters. The grimy man from my dreams, that is Parker's ancestor. Parker's sole duty in life was to kill me, and I am sure kill other witches. He forsook it, and his entire family just for me.

I haven't really stumbled into a huge witch community. It's very secretive. I know Henley and Valentina, the magic shopkeeper. I am not entirely sure she is a witch, but she definitely has a mystical quality about her and a vast knowledge of the magical arts.

I know eventually I will meet others like me. But I am not sure if all witches have my same circumstances. Do all witches have thousands of past lives? Do they remember them like Henley? Or live their current life with only clues and shadows from their past ones like me? Do they embrace the past, or do they try to carve out a new future? Do they have free will? Do I?

Clearly I am still struggling with this.

But my head and heart have been in a battle lately, and it's effecting my dreams. You see, sometimes the knight is clear. Sometimes I see Henley's smile, other times I hear Parker's laugh, the issue is- my dreams can't make up their damn mind. Parker one day, Henley the next, and sometimes like this one, I cannot tell anything at all.

I know this is a trivial problem compared to the rest of my life and to the world, but I know Parker and Henley need answers.

They are currently giving me "space." Their version of space consists of messaging Nicole constantly making sure I am okay, lurking just out of sight whenever I do venture out to grab my favorite coffee or treat, and I swear I sense them just outside of my apartment. I bet they even have worked out a rotation with one another. They practically are buddy buddy after joining forces to "save me".

Did their rescue plan utterly fail and they almost died themselves getting captured by Parker's witch hunter father? Did Nicole surprisingly save everyone's asses that day? Did she drive a truck literally into the murder barn? Yes, to all of the above. Hence the quotation marks on "save me"...

I have been working on finding my new normal. It's finally summer, so that means I get a break from classes, but I really am trying to buckle down to graduate sooner. So, I am debating taking a summer mini just to get some credits, but we shall see.

I see Nicole everyday, she is my next door neighbor and my best friend. She is also the only person, other than Parker and Henley, that knows I am a witch. She didn't take it well at first, but she is coming around. She now is just as naggy about me practicing my craft that she is about finishing my tea.

I see Liz every other day for brunch or lunch, and she probably knows I am keeping something from her, but I am waiting for the right time to tell her. I didn't do so well with Nicole, and Liz has become one of my best friends too. I almost lost Nic, I can't lose the people I love.

I still do magic lessons with Valentina, or I would if she would return my messages. She is a very mystical soul, and with that comes flightiness sometimes. It's been a few weeks since she's answered.

My plan is to go see her in person today and demand we get some lessons on the schedule. Knowing her, she will write them on her hand. I don't think she believes in calendars. With her being MIA lately, I have been doing some self study.

I can now without straining, lift up Puff, my familiar, much to her chagrin. We have even attempted communication, but not with much luck yet.

Apparently once witches and familiars' connection gets to the ultimate bond, they almost can read each other's minds. Puff makes her wants and needs really clear, but I do think she knows so much more than she is letting on about magic sometimes. I sometimes catch her eye when practicing the wording on spells, and I swear she knows I am doing something wrong. I want to be able to communicate with her, as long as its not just "pets please, wench"and "you got me the dry kibble again?!" Because right now, I feel as though her meows and attitude say that enough.

I turn over at look at the clock again. 5:30 am. I have been sitting with my thoughts for over two hours. There is no hope of going back to sleep. I guess I might as well start the day.

❖

Puff sits in her bed, tail twitching from left to right, as she watches Isabel get dressed for the day.

Puff watches over her while she sleeps, and tries to follow her even as Isabel leaves the comfort of the apartment.

The amount of times Puff has followed Isabel without her knowledge is truly astronomical. The few times she hasn't, that's when the bad things have happened. The two times Isabel was captured were days Puff felt off, she assumed it was the rat she found on the patio, but no, it was her gut telling her something was amiss.

She is learning just as Isabel is learning. But her instincts, she now knows, are never wrong.

Puff looks on, watching Isabel as she rounds up her things about to leave for the magic shop, probably after grabbing caffeine. Coffee is disgusting according to Puff, but Isabel drinks it religiously. Puff hates the walk to the coffee shop since there are always giant puddles she has to avoid. She also likes to give Isabel her pretend privacy, as the witch doesn't know how much Puff truly watches over her.

It is her familial duty. She no longer needs Isabel's blood to find her, though those love nips in the beginning truly forged their connection.

Puff can sense Isabel at all times, sense when she is in danger and can sense her presence. If the best friend didn't have the same psychic sense about Isabel, Puff was prepared to drag her by the ankle to the place Isabel was being kept with the two idiot males. Puff can sense a lot when it comes to the world around Isabel.

Puff knows something is about to change drastically for Isabel, she just hopes her sometimes aloof owner is ready for whatever it is.

CHAPTER 2

SURPRISE.

"Okay, Puffers. Try not to have too much fun without me." I tell Puff as I finally make my way to my door.

She eyes me and I swear I see the judgement in her eyes. Even though we cannot really communicate yet, I swear she is thinking something along the lines of, "Try not to die today, human."

So I answer as if that's what she really said- "I never try to die, Puff. Crazy dire circumstances keep seeking me out! But, today should be chill; I just am going to hound Valentina about magic lessons. She is flighty, but she's not dangerous."

Okay. Keys-check. Fanny-check. Emergency granola bar-check. I will be making a coffee run first though- I need my caffeine fix this morning. Heck who am I kidding- I need it every morning.

As I reach out to the door to open it, Puff dashes in front of me. I pull back, surprised at the sudden action. Puff is pretty calm most of the time. I don't think she leaves her bed a lot, at least not when I am here anyway.

"What's up Puff?" Wishing I truly had conquered the familiar communication.

Puff looks up at me, her blue and green eyes wide. I wait, not sure what is about to happen.

"Meorrrww."

"Um. I'm sorry, Puffers, I don't know what you want." I look around trying to guess what may be wrong.

"Ahh. I see- you're hungry," I spy the empty food bowl in the corner. I hurry and fill it up so that Puff will let me leave the apartment. I think the few times I have been captured kind of traumatized her when no one was here to feed her. Since Nicole now knows about me, I trust she will take over if it were to happen again. Not that its going to…but you know, good to be prepared. I quickly dart out the door before Puff can spot me again.

Puff looks up from her food at her owner as she leaves the safety of the apartment.

"Idiot human." Puff takes a few nibbles of her food, lets out what can only be described as a sigh of exasperation.

Then, the white ball of fur darts out her kitty door, onto the balcony, and jumps into the nearest tree. Ready for whatever comes her witch's way.

Sweet nectar of the gods in hand, also known as a caramel cold brew, I walk down the slowly waking street. It is still early morning, but no longer nocturnal creatures only time. Now it's the time of the roosters.

If Valentina's shop carried normal hours, I would be worried they wouldn't be open. However, she operates on witching hours, so the timing is a little different. Normal business hours are 9-5, but the magic shop is sporadic and spontaneous, like the owner herself.

While on the daily, it is open and operational from 7pm-3am, whenever I had a need for anything, it was always open and available to me.

I am pretty sure Valentina sleeps less than I do. Which is saying something...

I walk up to the door of the shop, and reach for the handle. I pause just before, a sense of something not right washing over me. A chill runs down my spine and I know instantly, Valentina is in trouble.

I pull open the door and rush inside, hoping I can save her before it's too late.

I look around in horror. The store is completely trashed. Bottles thrown on the floor, glass pieces everywhere. Pages from spell books littered all over the floor, torn from their binding. Crystals shattered on the counter, nothing at all like the neat rows and aesthetically pleasing arrangement they normally are in.

Taking in the glass counter, I shudder. Valentina's scarf she wears daily, sometimes as a headdress, a skirt, a shirt, or I have even seen her bind wounds with it- is ripped on the counter, laying in pieces.

I walk over slowly, fearing what I see as I move closer.

Tiny red flecks of blood line the colorful scarf, adding to its paisley pattern.

I am too late.

I reach for the scarf pieces, hands shaking.

I grab hold of the familiar fabric, pull it to my chest, just to feel closer to Valentina. As the fabric comes to my center, I am pulled into somewhere else altogether.

Valentina aligns her crystals in the way that makes her soul happy. They sometimes seem to speak to her, and request a different arrangement, but today they are silent.

She almost didn't open today, something felt not right with the air outside. But little Isabel needs her, and Valentina opened this shop to help witches just like Isabel, and to form connections with others like herself of course.

She was surprised when the famed Isabel walked in that first day, asking for dream supplies. Valentina immediately knew of her- the story of her many lives is one many witches speak of.

Many of her fellow witch kind seek out eternity, but after meeting Isabel, she knew it wasn't for her.

How sad must it be to have lived so much, and not truly lived a full life? She has had many lives, but none to remember and learn from. In the stories her kind shares, they always gloss over the fact she never lives longer than her twenties.

That is why when the boy came into her shop, many years ago when she was only an apprentice, and then again just this past year, she knew she would always help him and his lost love. Though romantic, their story makes her sad, for the both of them. Both cursed with memory, hers to forget, and his to remember.

Lost in memory, she perks up as the door's bells chime, as an older gentlemen strides in, a look a disgust on his face.

Many people often enter out of curiosity to her quaint shop, only a few have had hate in their hearts and shook her crystals in her faces. Most people have good in them, however, this man eyes her shop with pure hatred. She wants him out of here as soon as possible.

"Greetings, sir." She let her face fall into her shopkeeper smile, "How can I help you?"

He smiles then, and calling it a crocodile smile is a disservice to crocodiles. "I'm looking for a book."

He then runs over, before she has a chance to react, and slams her face into the glass countertop.

I come to, scarf still clutched to my chest. Shock rushing through me at what I just witnessed. I wouldn't call it a vision, because I wasn't just watching the scene unfold, I *was* Valentina, I could hear her thoughts.

My mind was racing, and trying to catch up with all I just discovered. I quickly went behind the shattered countertop, and grabbed where I knew Valentina stored pen and paper.

I need to visualize information to process it, and writing down things have always helped me.

-Valentina has been captured.
-He was looking for a book.
-the witch community knows about me.
-I don't ever live past my twenties.

When I saw the man through Valentina's eyes, even though she did not know who he was, I did. Parker's witch hunter father. Looking at the disaster around me, I now know why Valentina wasn't returning my messages. Guilt rushes through me-I feel bad for not investigating sooner. I should have known something was up.

That means that Mr. Hunting found Valentina after his failed capture attempt with me. I also have the feeling that whatever he is looking for in this book, has everything to do with killing me.

CHAPTER 3

LISTEN FIRST, REACT LATER

"Wait, wait, wait…slow down, Valentina is gone?" Zach is taking way too long to process everything when I instantly call him after leaving the magic shop.

"Yes! We have to go, we have to get her back, we have to do something!" The words pour out of me. I logically understand that we cannot do these things yet, but my logic is crushed by my reactionary heart. It wants to save her friend *now*.

"Take a breath, where are you?" He said, which I did take a long inhale before answering, trying to calm myself down.

"I just left the shop, I am currently pacing around the front, probably looking like a crazy person." I look around and confirm I have several sets of eyes staring at me.

"Go find somewhere you can calm yourself, and I will meet you there. Did you already tell Parker? Is he on the way?" Zach asked.

"No, Henley, you were the first one I called."

He is silent on the other end of the phone for a few brief moments.

"Okay, well, since it is his dad, we should loop him in."

"Whatever, just you both hurry up and get here. I am at my safe haven." I say frantically as I enter my favorite coffee shop. Maybe its magical coffee can make me feel better and calm down? I can't help Valentina if I am running around like a chicken with its head cut off- which is exactly what I was doing five minutes ago.

"Will do. And uh, Bel?" Zach said tentatively, "Thanks for calling me." He hangs up before I have a chance to respond.

After ordering the my second nectar of the gods of the day, I slide into a big booth by the wall. Did it mean something that I called Zach first? It's true, it is Parker's dad that captured Valentina, so it would have made sense I call him first? I called Zach because when it comes to all things witchy, especially Valentina, who he has known a lot longer than I thought, he is the expert.

I don't have time for this.

I pretend to look at the menu for food, even though one- I never stray from my usual, and two- eating sounds like the last thing I could do right now, my stomach is in knots. While I am pretending, someone walks up to the table. I hesitate to look up, feeling the presence, it truly could be anything with the kind of day I am having.

"Hey, hon, ready for our date?" I look up at the someone I was trying to ignore.

Scratch that- two someone's.

I look up and see my two best friends- Nicole and Liz. Crap. Our brunch date- I completely forgot. Nicole knows I am a witch, and could probably offer a lot of good insight into our current dilemma. But Liz doesn't know. She is truly the smartest woman I know, but I haven't told her about me yet.

It's hard to keep secret such a big thing about yourself, and have total fear that someone will hate you for it. Especially someone who I care about so much and means the world to me.

Being a witch isn't something I can change; I didn't choose this life to start, and I honestly have had times where I thought I could deny it into omission. But I can't, this is who I am. I am a witch. I now can't imagine a life without my powers, they are a part of me. Asking me to suppress my witch side is asking me to be only half of myself. I can't sacrifice this part of me for anyone, even if that person is one of my very best friends and basically my family.

Nicole has been babbling, talking about nothing, but just trying to fill the space. She glances over at me, knowing something is up, but also aware of the company we have.

Liz looks between both of us, her very best friends. She knows we have known each other forever, and at first she was afraid of becoming close with us. Like there wasn't room for her. Shit. I am reading her mind.

Liz thinks there is definitely something up. She made the choice to grow close to me, even though she knows there was always something different about me. I was worth the risk. She may not know the whole me, but she loves the parts I give her. She has learned that whether I decide to fully trust her or not, my friendship alone is enough.

Tears spring to my eyes. I can't do this. I have to tell her. I decide this is it. This is the moment I could possibly lose one of my best friends. I catch eyes with Nic, and she gives me a little smile, as if knowing what I am about to do.

"Iz, are you okay? You seem preoccupied, I mean, more than usual?" I let out a sigh. Liz can see right through me.

She continues- "You don't have to tell us anything, just know, and I speak for both of us," she says, turning towards Nicole, "that we will always be here for you."

The tears that were welling in my eyes start to fall. I take a breath and Nicole reaches over and squeezes my hand. She projects, *"You can do this."* Once we figured out the thought projection thing, it only brought us closer. I take a breath.

I squeeze her hand back and reach over with my other hand and grab Liz's hand.

"Liz, Nicole already knows this, but its really hard for me to talk about. It's a huge part of me, but it's also something that terrifies me." Liz smiles at me, nodding, willing me to continue. So I do.

"I am a witch." I lower my voice, aware we are in a public place. The world is not ready for me, I just hope Liz is. Nobody wants the chaos of the witch trials again. Least of all me-who actually lived through it. Kinda.

I wait for the rejection; for the pull away. I wait for Liz to run out screaming, or call the local psychiatric hospital and tell them to book me a room.

She doesn't do any of that.

Liz holds my hand a little tighter. "That must have been really hard. Thank you for trusting me."

Well, full on sobbing now. Thanks Liz.

With the emotional turmoil of the morning, and now Liz's complete understanding and acceptance, I am an emotional wreck.

"Isabel-what? Wait, my dad did he-" Parker ran to our table, seeing my distress and sensing the worst. Zach falling in behind him. Huh. Guess the buds carpooled. I blow my nose at the irony.

Nicole pats my hand and says, "Isabel was just getting Liz caught up on things. Can you both catch us up the rest of the way? Give our girl a break?" Thank the lord for my best friends.

Parker doesn't waste time. "Welcome to the gang, Liz." He flashes his winning smile before continuing.

"Well, Spark notes version- Isabel and Zach are both witches. I come from a family of witch hunters. My dad currently has napped the local friendly magic shop owner. He also probably has plans to kill all of us and take over the world. Wouldn't put it past him. Evil dude." Parker winks over at me. "Isabel Grace knows. But she'll get him. She always gets the bad guys."

I can't help it. I smile up at him. Even though he was the 'bad guy' at one point. I still very much doubt Parker would have gone through with killing me. I had to influence him to hang me on the noose, enacting my escape plan. I still feel the guilt radiating from him a year later. We need to talk. I need to tell him I am over it, and he should be too. He has saved my life since then- and risked his own for mine.

Zach looks between Parker and me, furrowing his brow and shaking his head. He steps forward and says, "Come with me, I have an idea."

CHAPTER 4

PARKER'S VIEW.

I hate this. My freaking dad couldn't leave well enough alone. I look over at Isabel as she listens to Zach's plan. He just came right out of the gate with a plan to fix it all, didn't he?

It's my dad. I should be the one with all the ideas. Why did I feed into all the bullshit he told me my whole life? I still can't believe I almost...I look over at Isabel again. She meets my eyes, and smiles at me. A smile full of forgiveness and grace, a smile I shouldn't deserve.

We are at the magic shop, and seeing what he is capable of makes me shudder.

I mean, I've seen him torture people he thought were witches, heck, he tortured me. But he still taught me how to ride a bike; he showed me how to change a tire. He also showed me which artery to cut in the neck to keep someone alive but bring them to the edge of death.

I may have been the ideal student, but I didn't have the mentality. My brother was the idiot, but he was bendable. Dad says jump off a cliff, he says, "Yes, sir. Should you push me off?" My brother during initiation didn't hesitate to kill someone. Meanwhile, I fell in love with my witch.

Yep. I love Isabel Grace.

I was scouting her out from the very first day of school. We suspected she was the rumored witch that had eluded my family. We were taught how she goes against everything we stand for. Every time we took her life, and every time she came back was a direct insult to my family's legacy. As if she has a choice in the matter.

We weren't sure though if she was the same girl- she seemed so different, not a magic thought in her. But when I saw the dream book, I knew. I knew I couldn't put it off any longer.

Every time she bumped into me, I loved having her in my arms. I loved the way her body shuddered. I know it was probably her witchy instincts warning her about a hunter, but her body was *reacting* to me. I knew she liked me, from the few times she worked up her courage to talk to me.

I would see her straighten her shoulders, take a deep breath, and then proceed to ask me- "So, what is your favorite form of potato?" Something ridiculous like that, and cute. It was easy to fall for her. But the day I took her, goes down as the hardest day of my life.

I drugged her, tied her up, I pictured all the different ways I could kill her. Now, I know she can read minds, so she saw that too. She knows what I am capable of. What could have happened to her, with the noose I put around her neck.

I walk away from the Scooby gang. I can't pretend this isn't all my fault. I am a hunter. I come from a line of hunters. I am the only one who can stop my father. No matter what happens to me, she will be safe. If my father is desperate enough to turn to magic, he is dangerously desperate.

"Parker Hunting."

I turn at the sound of my name to see the most beautiful woman rushing after me. I really could get lost in her eyes. Isabel runs over to me, grabbing my arm, and giving it a tight squeeze. I guess she wants to say goodbye. I will allow myself one guilty pleasure before I die. I reach for her hand, shocked when she smacks me with the same hand she was just using to squeeze my arm.

"Don't you dare do what I think you're going to do." Her intense eyes stare at me. "You cannot sacrifice yourself for me. One- it may not work and I will *not* lose you to your father. Two- there is now magic involved. So we have find out what spell he is going to cast. To do that- I need to reach Valentina."

"I need to save you. That's the only way you could ever forgive me for-"

She cuts me off- "Shut your mouth about me forgiving you. That is done and has been done since the very night you captured me. Parker- I willed you to hang me. You were not stable and I knew I needed to take you out of the equation." She doesn't give me a chance to deny her. "You have no idea how many times you have saved me. Even before all of this, you would save me everyday you smiled at me. Every lame joke, every time you truly saw me- you saved me. We are even."

She pauses, and I think she's finished. I struggle and try to think of what to say. But she takes a shaky breath in and says, "You are whoever you want to be Parker Hunting. You are not your family." She wraps her arms around me.

I don't know if I believe her. But her saying it, I want it to be true. I don't think I deserve her forgiveness, but after a moment, I can't help but wrap my arms around her. We stay there, embraced for what was probably just ten seconds, but it truly felt like time stopped.

Zach, Nicole, and Liz may have been in the same room, but to me, there was just us. Isabel and me. Witch and witch hunter.

Well, I guess I'm retired. If that was ever really going to be an option for me, with or without meeting Isabel.

I'm just a hunter.

I have a pretty good idea who I am hunting next.

CHAPTER 5

TIME TO ACT.

I lay in bed thinking about the plan. Zach was spot on, as always. He knew right away what to do- a location spell. Find Valentina, then use my ability to read minds to find out more information, like what spell is Mr. Hunting going to cast.

I want to save Valentina and go in guns blazing like Parker, but I know that Mr. Hunting is messing with magic. Without knowing exactly what we are walking into, we could walk straight into a booby trap.

However, the more I think on the plan, the more holes I find. Mostly concerning my part- which is the main part of the plan. If I can't communicate with her telepathically, we're screwed.

When I tried to read Zach's mind, he immediately shot me down, at the time saying I couldn't because he was a witch too. How could I possibly read Valentina's?

Also, other than influencing Parker, I have never communicated back with the mind I am reading. It has always been a one way path, not a two way line. I can hear, but I have never tried speaking.

I know Zach is going to kill it with the location spell, he is the expert. He is good at everything he does.

I just hate I happen to be the mind reading expert. Zach says he can feel intentions, but only sometimes, nothing like the entire storylines I get when reading minds. He says in every life, telepathy has always been my strongest power.

I guess we will put that to the test tomorrow night.

I just hope it works…I don't trust that Parker will let us have another chance to fix this. I knew he wanted to save the day, and risk it all. The fact that he thinks his actions are unforgivable shock me. How could someone with so much good think the worst in themselves?

When we spoke earlier, it truly felt as there was just us in the room. It wasn't until we broke apart and I locked eyes with Zach that guilt filled me. His hurt eyes and Nicole's knowing smile made me jump about ten feet back.

I technically do not owe either of them anything, at least not in this life.

Zach has loved me in every lifetime, can he just give me time to catch up? Do I even want to? I care about both of them so much.

A quiet knock on the door breaks me out of my thoughts. Puff looks up, then falls back asleep.

I trust her instincts, and know it must be a friend. Probably Nicole, locked out of her apartment once again after a night out. It wouldn't be the first time she has crashed at my place.

I open the door, ready to make some sarcastic comment to my best friend.

"Hey, Bel. Can I come in?"

Um. Not Nicole. Green eyes, sandy blonde hair covering them, and the kindest of smiles greet me at the door.

"Zach…of course-is everything okay? Is it Valentina?" I step aside and let him in.

"No, everything's fine, at least, nothing has changed." He quickly assures me, "I just needed to see you." I wait, knowing there's more to come. There always is with Zach.

"I feel like I haven't given you a chance, you know, to know me. I turned your world upside down, then left you alone to figure things out. I thought giving you space was the right thing to do, but it wasn't. Things make more sense when were together Bel, they always have." He grabs my hands and leads me to the couch. He sits, pulling me down with him.

"I know you're antsy about the plan, so first off, talk to me. I'm here." He pauses, willing me to go on.

"I can't even read your mind, how could I read Valentina's? How can I communicate with her? I have barely been a witch for a year, I don't think I can do this." I pull my hands away from him and look down at my lap, ashamed to meet his eyes.

"Bel, look at me-" he gently raises my chin to meet his eyes. I can see in his beautiful green eyes that he has complete and utter faith in me. "Read my mind."

So I do. I see me. Through Zach's eyes.

I see me sitting on my couch but I also see another me from fifty years ago, on a different couch. I see every me, through his eyes. No matter what time, his love never fades.

Every life, he has to earn my trust and love. I never remember him, but he loves the journey. He thinks it's like falling in love over and over again. He views it as his greatest adventure.

He is sad that he has made the wrong choices with me. He wishes he found me sooner. He realizes since my family isn't a huge part of my life, he should have been here long ago. Helping me along the way, through every bad dream and maybe then we wouldn't be fighting witch hunters.

Maybe there would be no Parker to deal with, though he's not such a bad guy. Just annoying the way Parker looks at me, and touches me. Does he know I am meant to be with Zach? He starts to think of the initial spell that caused our lives to forever be intertwined and wishes…

All of a sudden, I am shut out. But not before a huge wave of pure love washes over me.

"Woah. I think you saw more than I meant. See I told you-you're good. I can purposely block you Iz, but if I didn't see you coming, you would go through all my walls instantly. The same should happen with Valentina. She also is more of a teacher than a true practitioner. She likes to guide others rather than cast herself, unless absolutely necessary."

I take a breath, maybe I can do this. Though I do have a lot of questions, I take a breath to ask one, but before I can start…

"Before you even ask, let's experiment. Try to communicate with my mind."

I close my eyes. This is what I wanted, but now that we're here, I am scared. Zach takes my hands and I feel the encouragement, even though I can't see him. His belief and support just fills me up, so I mentally reach to him.

"What spell did we cast together?" The biggest question I have wondered since meeting him- why are we like this?

He sighed, and I know it worked. He lets go of my hand with one hand, holding the other one tightly. His hand reaches up to cup my face, gently rubbing his thumb across my cheek. I wait, knowing this is hard for him. I know he is afraid I will run away. Maybe a year ago Isabel would have, but I have seen too much since then. I don't scare off as easily.

"Back then, every day we had together was a gift. People could die from a paper cut, much less with mass hysteria going on about witches. The amount of innocents hurt and killed was terrifying to be witness to. We knew it was a scary time, and wanted to do everything we could to stay together. So, we took action."

His hand drops from my face and he releases my hand. He stands up and takes a few steps towards the window, lost in memory.

"You've already seen how you were taken- by Hunting's ancestor. You escaped, but we knew that that was just luck. So we made up a spell that was meant to keep us safe and together. This wasn't something that had been done before, but blood magic is the most powerful, that we knew. You were already covered in cuts and bruises, so I volunteered. I think that is what makes me remember everything, it's my blood that powered the spell, so I have the upper hand." He looks behind at me with guilt. I don't think memory is the upper hand here though. I am thankful for my lack of heartbreak.

"I sliced my hand open, and we sealed it with a kiss. Blood magic is most powerful, but love topples everything else. The combination of the two resulted in a spell we couldn't have imagined. We find each other in every life, and love one another for the rest of our days. Then, it starts over again." He gives me a small smile then turns back towards the window. He is glossing over an important item.

I mentally send, *"Why do I always die?"* He turns around sharply. *"Valentina's thoughts told me at the shop. I never make it past my twenties."* I couldn't say it aloud. But it has been gnawing at me all day.

"Isabel... I... I don't know. I have read every book I can on reincarnation and souls, and I cannot for the life of me figure out why you never survive. All I want is to grow old with you, and all I ever do is watch you die-". His voice cracks on the last word and he falls to his knees.

I rush over to him. Not only can I see the anguish he feels, but I see it in his mind. Every time my life ends, and every time he falls in pieces. The amount of times he has seen me die, flashes all at once.

The ways I have died are different, some supernatural and others natural, but one thing is always the same. Henley holding on to me, and there for the very end. Just like I am holding on to him now.

Our eyes meet, his green eyes still full of tears. I normally see them full of laughter and joy, but now there is only despair. The things he has seen...how can he have so much happiness when he has seen so much?

But then it comes to me. How he does it every time and what is going to pull him out right now.

I gently grab his face just as he had held mine five minutes ago. I rub the stubble on his jaw, all the while, our eye contact never breaking.

"Henley...You must live in this moment, right here. With me...I'm here. I'm not dead, so be with me... in *this* moment." He gently grabs hold of my wrists, slowly pulling them down to the floor.

He leans closer, I feel his shaky breath as his face draws closer to mine.

Closer- until he is only an inch away from my lips.

Then, he stops. His eyes flicker from my mouth to meet my eyes, asking permission.

I don't wait. I close the distance and practically slam my mouth into his. Reaching around his head, pulling him closer, barely stopping to come up for air.

His arms wrap around my waist, pulling me in tighter, my knees sliding against the carpet. I silently curse that I didn't splurge and get the fuzzy rug I was eyeing at Target.

As we kiss, I just get a sense of rightness; like this is where I should be. Tangled in his arms, protected by my hero, just like I always have been, in every life. I may not remember it exactly, but my soul and body definitely are in agreement right now- I belong here.

CHAPTER 6

SPELLS, POWERS, FAMILIARS, OH MY.

I'm back. The domain of so many of my nightmares, the place I used to think was Hell. My past. I look around- I don't see the flames, the grimy old man, no angry villagers. I don't even see Zach- just an empty quiet village at night.

I squint in the shadows, seeing someone approach. If its like my previous dreams, its possible its Zach or Parker.

But I don't need to be rescued.

"Good Morrow, Isabel. I thought we should convene with one another."

Stepping out of the shadows, into the light, is me.

Well, not me exactly. But the me from this time, the original Isabel; who started it all.

"Um. Hi. What's up." I awkwardly respond. She then looks up at the night sky, not understanding me.

"Tis' night- but the stars do look lovely, do they not? I wanted to tell you, that thou are correct." She stares intently at me, willing me to understand.

"Right about...? That bananas taste better a little smooshed? No, that doesn't seem right...". I see her look of confusion before she continues. Curse my randomness, not the time brain. Focus.

"No, you're right about what you told your Zachary...And your Parker." Whoah. Bringing up both my boys...

Well, I guess one of them is hers, too... This is weird.

"I have had a lot of good conversations lately, can you help me a little more?" I push- I cannot handle her riddles right now.

"You said to Parker, 'You are whoever you want to be' and your words to Zachary were, 'Live in the moment'. Why do you not follow your own advice, sister? You do not have to be bound unless you wish to be- you are powerful. More than I am, more that anyone you know. But you must embrace your power and yourself fully. Only then, can you live as you truly desire...with who you desire."

She starts to blur and reality starts to claim me.

"Wait" I cry, "I still have so many questions for you!"

She smiles, "Goodbye, sister." A sad smile is the last thing I see when it all goes black.

❖

I wake on the living room floor, gently pull myself from Zach's arms. I don't want to wake him up, and I know I am a mess after that strange dream. He would see my face and immediately want to know what was up.

What did past me mean? Take my own advice? I thought I was just a victim of fate? Of the choices *she* made? I thought Zach was the only answer. The only option. I look over at him, as I grab my clothes for the day stashed in my room. He looks so peaceful, how can I ruin that?

She also only talks to me and sends visions when something big is about to happen. While my love life is pretty dramatic, I do not think it's worth sending visions across hundreds of of years over. There must be something else.

Did it seem like she was saying goodbye? For forever?

I quietly feed Puff so she doesn't nag Zach awake and I slip out the door. More questions than answers, as usual when it comes to my dreams.

I need some time alone. Sure, I proved I can communicate Zach mentally. But when I literally have Valentina's life counting on me, can I still handle it? It's not just her life either, it could be my life or lives at stake too, and who knows what else.

I figure the coffee shop is good place to be alone, since it's early, and most of my crew don't start waking up until at least the sun is awake.

I quietly slip out the door, sliding out, careful not to make any sudden movements, tip toeing in to the hallway.

I nearly jump out of my skin when I hear a chuckle in front of me.

"Good morning, chica."

Okay, so Nicole scared the tar out of me. She is normally a night owl.

"Nic!" I shout whisper at her. "You scared me! Why the heck are you awake right now?" The creeper is just leaning against her door, hands behind her back, and she gives me a small smile.

"Trust me, I will be going back to sleep soon. I just woke up a few minutes ago, and wanted to give you this". She reveals that she has a to-go cup behind her back. I immediately smell her lavender green tea mix she makes herself.

I feel a smile start on my own face, "That sounds perfect Nic." I reach out for the cup, and she grabs my hand, still keeping the cup into her chest with the other hand.

"I also wanted to tell you, that you truly can do anything, Bel. I know you doubt yourself, but witch or not, anything you set your mind to do, you can do. You just have to believe in yourself as much as we do." She gives my hand an extra squeeze then slides the to-go cup into my hands and wraps hers around mine. She leans in a little closer, like she has a secret.

"Bel-I love you, babe." She then turns to go back inside her apartment, I assume to get a little bit more sleep.

"Wait- Nicole, how did you know? I...I have been stressing about things lately, and you- how do you always know?"

I hate asking for help. I like to think I have gotten better, but honestly, I just have gotten better at using my powers and not getting such bad side effects. They have made an already independent woman, even more independent. Which doesn't really benefit me, since sometimes, even witches need help. I mean, help as in exactly what Nicole did for me, just full, unconditional support.

"I always do know, with you especially. I'm not sure, I just woke up and knew you would need me today. Same feeling happened when you were captured, and when your high school boyfriend dumped you over a text message. I just get this urge to be with you. I get it about other things too, but its always been strongest with you. I guess I have really good intuition or something. Night- I am going to bed like the rest of the world is currently." With that- she goes back inside.

Um. So, am I just hyper sensitive to the subject, or is Nicole displaying witchy abilities?

I shake it off, knowing we don't have time for this, but definitely something to experiment with later. I take a small sip of the tea and immediately feel ten times better. She truly is magical, whether she is a witch or not.

I walk into the coffee shop, seeing a quick flash of white in my peripheral vision, and I throw away Nicole's now empty to-go cup. Yes, I just finished a whole cup of tea. Yes, I am about to get a sugary coffee beverage. Deal with it.

The tea healed my mind, and the nectar of the gods will heal my soul.

It's still early, but I can always count on this place being open when I need it. I love coming here when the world is still waking up. I get the whole place to myself, and…I get my favorite table. I walk towards my favorite place to sit when I am by myself, wanting to put my stuff down before I order.

Except this time…it's not empty. Ugh. I wish I could keep a reserved sign on it. I have asked. They said no. Something about I am not the only customer. Whatever.

I walk closer and squint, trying to see in the dim lighting who dared steal my designated table. Definitely feeling a sense of Deja vu from when I first met Zach…

"Sup Bel." Hazel eyes and a smirk that used to make me melt greet me. Ha. Who am I kidding? 'Used to'? I still melt every time I see him.

Parker Hunting is sitting at my table, in my favorite coffee place. He even has my favorite drink waiting at the seat next to him. Ugh.

I angrily grab the cup from him and take a seat. Grrr.

"Holdup- did you just growl at me?" He laughs and looks over at me semi shocked at my animalistic noises.

"Yep. I'll do it again too if you keep stealing my table." I glare at him then take a sip of the best coffee I will ever have. I sigh and close my eyes, "That's the stuff."

Parker laughs and shakes his head, "Guess you just needed your fix for the day? Well, it was my pleasure to oblige." He did a little sweep of his arm, like a bow.

I glare at him some more, then say. "Thank you. Um, so... did you come here to chat or did you just happen to order my favorite drink in my favorite place coincidentally?"

His laughing smirk fell as he looked down at his hands, almost sheepishly. "I knew you'd be here, because well, you're always here. I just wanted to do something for you. I feel like you've done so much for me."

I start to argue, what have I done other than make his life more complicated?

He cuts me off and raises his hand, pleading me to wait- "You changed my life, Isabel. The path I was on...it wouldn't have ended with me as a good guy. Now, because of you... because I want to be better for you, I see myself as someone who could be good." He drops his hand, allowing me to finish.

"Parker. How many ways and times do I have to tell you- You. Are. Good. Why else would I-". I stop, not even sure what I was about to say.

Whatever I was about to say, Parker liked it. He smiled and took my hand. I pulled away, knowing I needed to be upfront with him. I did just spend the night with Zach. Not that anything like *that* happened. But we did kiss- a lot. We fell asleep in each other's arms, and I was fully ready to commit to him, until the whole dream sequence made me question everything.

"Hold the phone, Parker Hunting. One- there is a lot going on at the moment, and you can't just use those eyes and smile at me, expecting me to drop everything and be with you. Two- I need to tell you something. Um...Me and Henley have kissed... a few times actually." How do I not downplay what me and Henley have gone through? Who knows what we have done in past lives- I assume everything. I assume I have given my whole heart to him, I know he has to me. Guilt starts... but before it gets too far Parker drops my hand.

"One-" He holds up a finger, mimicking me. "I know there is a lot happening, but something I have learned is you have to take hold of things while you still have them. So that's what I am doing- I am holding on to you, as tight as I can. And two-" He holds up a up a second finger, the smirk slowly taking over his face. "What's fair is fair, Bel. If you kissed him, shouldn't I have a chance too?"

I pause. Thinking of all the reasons this is *not* a good idea.

Parker is clearly dealing with lots of emotions right now- well, I guess I am too...

I apparently may not have that much time left.

I have a complicated relationship with Zach-spanning decades, and I just spent the night with him. But I have wanted something with Parker ever since I first met him at school. I shiver when I think of the finger grazes back when we first met. Now he is wanting to kiss me? How did this even happen?

I try again, "Parker, I just want to make sure you understand. Me and Henley have history, I am not even sure of what all has happened between us, I just want to make sure you know exactly what you are signing up for. I...I'm not even sure what I want and who exactly I am still." I pull away; no one is crazy enough to stay with that I have going on.

"I know exactly who you are- Isabel Grace. The girl of my dreams." He smiles and I can't help it- I smile back. Dreams and me, we go way back.

"I like Zach, I really do. But I just want to even the playing field. He's had years on me, can't I get just get one kiss?"

He stops, and his whole flirty demeanor drops. "Even if it's a goodbye kiss, Isabel. I would get it. I will honor whatever choice you make, and stand by you. No matter what."

Well, that was all it took. I am a sucker for supportive men, and I seem to be surrounded by them.

I lean in this time, not giving him a chance to change his mind about me. My lips softly brush against his, lightly brush once, then another. I pull back, mentally asking if he's okay. He is still.

"Isabel Grace, I am more than okay." He answers. Oh. Did I mean to do that?

He then cups his hands around my face and pulls me in, his lips crashing into mine. Still gentle, testing the waters, the intensity starts to build the more comfortable we are with the kiss. The shiver starts up my spine and my shoulders shake a little, never breaking from the kiss. He smiles against my mouth, as if he knows he is the only one who does this to me. I should start calling it the Parker Tingle.

He slowly breaks away and gives my nose a delicate peck. he runs a fingertip up and down my arm, barely grazing my skin. Oh my goodness, I am going to die from the sensations. I can't muffle the shiver this time; I roll my head as it turns into a full out shake. He leans in close to my neck, softly breathing me in. I inhale shakily, thinking this can't get more intense than that.

"I love the way your body reacts to me" He whispers magnetically into my ear. I lean away shyly, hyper sensitive and to a point of almost ticklish in response.

He doesn't leave my neck, instead he starts to kiss from my ear, all the way down to my shoulder. I start to close my eyes, and he gently skims his mouth down. I start to anticipate his touch, and every time his lips reach my skin, it feels like sparks on the edge of my skin.

A throat clears behind me. The barista is looking at the two of us accusingly. *Get a room you two.* Oops. According to her thoughts, she is not too happy with us. I muffle out an excuse to Parker and run out the door. Once again, more confused than I was before.

CHAPTER 7

LOCATION, LOCATION, LOCATION.

I texted Zach, asking him to meet me early at the magic shop. I wanted to prep for the location spell, but I also felt like he deserved to know what went down with me and Parker. Ugh. I am the worst.

I walk in to the place that has become a second home to me. I remember how out of place I felt when I walked into the magic shop the first time. Valentina knew I was meant to meet her, and I just thought she was a weirdo.

I now know, I'm the weirdo. Honestly, biggest thing that has changed this year since finding out I am a witch- I'm proud of who I am.

When I was 'ordinary', I never thought I was worth knowing. Now witch or not, I know I matter.

I always thought that people didn't want to know me, they just wanted to know Nicole, or needed help with an assignment. I now wonder if I just wasn't giving people a chance by just assuming I wasn't worth it. Maybe they did want to know me, and I just didn't give anyone the option.

I look over at the person who changed my mindset about myself. Who has complete and utter faith in me, no matter how many times he's seen me fail. Whose love for me has stood the test of time and seems to have a never ending cap of patience for my shenanigans. Who has embraced my friends as his own because he knows they are more like family. Who gives his whole heart to me, and opened up his soul for me to see.

Who woke up this morning with his arms empty.

Whose heart I am about to break.

I am a horrible person.

His eyes meet mine, and I don't see anything but love look back at me. He's been cleaning up the shop, trying to make it seem less disastrous in here for me. His eyes crinkle as he smiles, the 100 watt smile that haunted me for days after I first met him.

I'm stuck. I take a breath, knowing I'm about to ruin everything.

"Morning, Bel. I had a good time last night, I mean if good is enough of a word for last night. Ha." He laughs to himself sheepishly. "I'm not even talking about the physical stuff, I mean of course that was amazing, you're amazing. But I mean the other stuff, the talking."

Shit. Guilt pours over me. I kissed two boys who mean the world to me. I am a horrible, horrible person. One horrible just isn't enough for me.

I take another breath, hyping myself up.

"Bel, I am going to stop you right there. Whatever you are about to admit doesn't matter." Wait, what? I'm shocked.

"I mean, well it does, but it doesn't take away from what we shared. I opened up to you and we connected on a deeper level, not just physically. Our souls joined." He smiles and once again, I'm dumbstruck by how beautiful he is.

He continues- "I know you felt it too- a sense of rightness, of belonging. That's our souls. When we join up, it's like it always has been, our souls connect and we are meant to be. They know it and we know it."

It's really weird to think of our souls as a they…mainly to personify it at all. How do souls have opinions of their own? But I guess that goes back to the original spell OG Isabel and Zach cast, that our souls would always be joined. My soul is acting of its own accord. Huh. I hate that.

"Henley," I say his last name out of the love I do have for him, hoping it'll make what I am about to say hurt less.

"I need you to understand, I do care for you, so, so much. But, I am not my soul. I thought we were the same, but I am not sure. Past Isabel made me see that…". His face grows confused at that. "I care for you both, you and Parker, and I just don't think it's fair to all that's riding on us to worry about our relationships right now. Just know, I do love you,". His eyes light up, "Just I don't know in what way just yet. I need to figure out what I want vs. what my soul wants." He nods slightly and then turns away, pretending to look busy.

He clears his throat, "Ahem, okay well is it just going to be us for the spell?"

"Not on your life, witch." Parker walks in, signature smirk on his face, my two best friends behind him in tow.

"Good morning guys, I want to make it clear- If I am just getting in the way, please tell me. I don't want to overstep, I have faith in you, and I just wanted to support." Liz says quickly, knowing she is out of her element.

"Nonsense, babe. We are here for Iz. No one could pull us away. She needs us- not these stinky boys." Nicole always knows what to say to lighten the mood, but also she's totally right. If it was just me and my guys, my head would be somewhere else. Thinking of their arms around me, their hands pulling my hair, their lips...Hold on. Off topic...

I shake my head, trying to pull my thoughts out of the gutter. Nicole has her eyes on me, and she stares at me knowingly. She then thinks at me, "Ooo girl. You got dirt. Well, save it for later. Clean up your mind dirty bird."

I look over at Zach, raising my brows at him and project over- "Ready for this?"

He says aloud- "I"m ready. Are you?"

Am I? I have to be.

Zach wasn't just cleaning the store earlier, he was getting out the materials.

He walks us through the spell. We all have to have our intentions set clear, magic or no.

"First, we need a possession of Valentina's, something dear to her. I, uh, picked some crystals from her personal collection. She always has swore they are a part of her and has always tried to get me to use them more." A collection of rocks, I mean crystals, are on top of the repaired glass countertop. I guess Zach also fixed that. I make eye contact with him. "I just didn't want her to come home with everything trashed. ". He looks away, never one to steal attention from the task at hand.

"What exactly is everything? I did some basic research just to prepare." Of course, she did. Liz is the smartest woman I know.

Zach picks up a stone, a purple swirl, smooth to the touch. "This is amethyst." I grab it from his hand, rubbing my thumb across the smooth surface.

"Yes- that's supposed to help with dreams and sleep right?" Liz quotes from her photographic memory.

"Um. Excuse me, it helps with dreams?" What the heck. Where was this last year? Valentina never mentioned...ugh. I guess I didn't ask the right questions.

I groan and set it down. "What about this one?" An orangey reddish stone seems to be pulsating, emitting an energy stronger than the others. It has a mosaic look, beautiful in its brokenness. I pick it up, rolling it around in my hand. It definitely feels like its what we are looking for.

"Brecciated Jasper, I believe." Liz answers, looking over at Zach for approval. He smiles and nods.

"Exactly, Liz. Nice." His approval shines and she smiles back. A flash of something goes thru me. Calm down, Iz. "It's known for strength and grounding the user. Randomly, it's also known for communication with familiars..." He looks over at me with a small smile.

Where have these crystals been all my life? Where was Puff when I needed her? At the thought, I swear I see a flash of white for the glass door. Nah. Couldn't be. Puff is asleep in her sunny spot right about now.

"I will definitely be using this later then." I hand it back over to Henley. "But it does feel right for what we need... don't you think?" I ask the group uncertainly.

"If it feels right to you Bels, then it must be right." Nicole smiled at me and gave me a reassuring nod. I look around at the people who I consider family, feeling and hearing their support shining at me. They all believe I can do this.

"Okay then. Let's get to saving the day." I look over to Henley, nodding at him to continue.

He smiles in pride at me, then says, "Okay, so we have the item connected to Valentina." He rolls out the map on the glass countertop, its of our city and surrounding areas. The back part of my mind thinks- where did he find a map? Do they still sell maps? Focus. "We all will need to connect with the map, hands on the edges, while Iz holds her hand over the stone."

I look up sharply from the map at him. He projects to me- *You have to be connected to her for the communication to work. It only makes sense you're the conduit for this. But I will be here the whole time with you.*

He continues aloud- "She will think of Valentina, starting off in the center of the map. We all will channel Valentina into our thoughts and Isabel should feel pulled to her location. From there, the communication pathway should be open."

"I am hearing a lot of 'shoulds' and not it will happen" Parker says, eyebrows raised.

"Magic is never a definite, Hunting." Zach responds.

"But Isabel is a definite, Zachary." Parker says with force, not even looking at me.

"Okay, Okay, my guys, we can get out the measuring stick later, I volunteer as judge." Nicole jokes and Liz just laughs and shakes her head. At least her joke smoothed the tension, I still feel it between the two men, almost as if there is a solid line between the three of us.

"You are right about one thing, Hunting. Isabel can definitely do this." He smiles at me, then folds the crystal into my hands, backing up to where he can palm the edge of the map. Everyone else starts to follow suit. Hands on the map, closing their eyes, I look around at my friends. Now it is my turn.

I move the crystal to the center of the map, closing my eyes and thinking of Valentina.

I keep imagining my hands moving, just like it's some Ouija board game, but I still them making sure they are available to move on their own accord.

I think of the kooky shopkeeper. Her smile, her bohemian attire, scarves galore, her fair olive skin, her deep brown eyes, full of kindness, her patience, her guidance, and her love. I hold on to her crystal and focus everything I can on the amazing woman who chose to help me. I will find her, there is no other option. She will be alive, she is strong.

She is a bad ass witch, and she will not let a puny man destroy her. Mainly because if he destroys her, he can get to me.

I'm there! I gasp- keeping my eyes closed, not wanting to break the connection.

"That's it- now let her guide you." Henley says, but my fingers were already moving on their own, almost as if she was sliding them herself. My hands move slowly across the map, before coming to stop. I am afraid to move, not wanting to break the connection.

"We got her, Isabel Grace, you did it." Parker says, and I know he's smiling. He may be afraid of his father, but he is still proud of me.

"You did great, Bels, keep holding on." Nicole knows that was the easy part.

"Keep reaching, Isabel, you're almost there." Liz says, but her voice is fading. I no longer am in the magic shop. I don't feel my family around anymore.

I slowly open my eyes, pain filling my body.

One eye will not fully open, as if it is swollen shut. I clutch my arm to my chest, waiting for the dreams to take me, before my nightmare returns.

CHAPTER 8

HE IS THE NIGHTMARE.

I did it. I am in Valentina's mind.

But I am just a passenger- I am Valentina, not Isabel right now. I just can witness what happens to her.

After all that work, I can't tell her I am here to save her.

Valentina is severely injured from what I can sense. She can't open her right eye, her arm is broken, possibly her shoulder as well. Knife slits run down her leg, almost like it was teasing her. She is curled up on the wet, damp floor, trying to find escape in her dreams. It hurts like hell.

She flinches when the door slams, sprawling back as far away as her broken body can. Her nightmare enters.

"Hello, witch. I see you still haven't been able to heal yourself. Pity. That was making it more fun in the beginning." Mr. Hunting strides in, a spell book under his arm. "Guess that last spell really did a number on you, huh?" He takes out the book from under his arm, opening it and reads, "Weakening Spell- weakens your enemies, making them vulnerable." He slams the book shut, face nearing Valentina's. She shakes but doesn't move away, looking him in the eye. Good job, Valentina.

"Your kind" he spits at her "uses this on my family, on innocent people. How does it feel for your own spell to be used on you?"

"You are not innocent. You are a evil creature." Valentina then actually spits on his face that was inches away from hers.

She may know what was about to happen, but I was not prepared when he smacked her into the damp floor. Pain rushes through me, feeling everything she feels.

"You bitch. I am so ready to be done with you. My patience is wearing thin. You will help me cast this spell, and then you will beg me for your death." He grabs her and painfully drags her over to the light in the room.

He opens the book and slams her face till its inches away from the book. "We are doing this. Tonight. Better get ready. Your little witch won't know what hit her." He grabs the book and starts to leave, thinks better of it, turning around to face her.

I look up at him with hatred, in Valentina's eyes. His boot crashing down at her face is the last thing I see before it goes black.

❖

I no longer feel I am in Valentina's mind. I look down at my hands, I can move, they are MY hands. I look around and still am in the grimy room she was being kept in. Is it a basement of some sort? The floor is damp all over, and it feels musky, almost as if we are by the water.

"Hello, dear. I have been waiting for you." I look over in surprise, Valentina is here, and she can see me.

"We know where you are and we are coming Valentina. I am so sorry, but we will save you."

She reaches for me, and in the light of the dream, I can't see her injuries. She is whole.

"My time is drawing near, but I needed to talk to you while we were still connected."

She knew I was connected to her? Wait, her time is near?

"NO. We will save you. This is my fault." Tears start to rush down my face.

She grabs my face in her hands pulling me in close, "You did not ask for any of this, Isabel. I know that and you should too. You have had no control in this life or the others. That is what I need to talk to you about."

There is so much I want to say, but I can sense her readiness to speak.

"This spell alone will not kill you. But he means to cast it, and then you will be vulnerable to death."

'Oh yeah, I saw what he did to you, the weakening spell, right?"

"Hush, no. That was so I would stop fighting back, he wants to do so much worse to you." I wait, preparing for what is to come.

"First, he will cast the spell that will sever you from your lives, making it to where if you die, you cannot come back. Then, he will kill you. For good."

I start to sense my surroundings at the magic shop. Shit.

"What do you mean sever me from my lives?" I ask, knowing I am about to wake up.

"He wants to break the spell you and Zachary cast so many lives ago. So that when you die, he will have finally won."

"Isabel Grace, come on… come back to me." I hear voices pulling me back to my own body and mind.

"Iz…babe, wake up-you're freaking me out."

"Isabel…I need you." Henley's voice is what finally pulls me out. I slowly open my eyes. I am no longer standing and holding the map. I am on the ground of the magic shop, with everyone around me, with worried looks on their faces.

"You are not doing that again- that was freaking scary." Nicole tackles me into a hug.

"Oof. I'm okay, Nic." I awkwardly pat her arm from my laying down position.

Both Parker and Henley extend a hand towards me- offering to help me up. Honestly, after traveling miles away to someone else's mind, I could use all the help I could get.

I reach for both of them. I give Parker my left hand, and Henley my right, and together they pull me up to standing. But before they could do anything, Liz intercepts.

She stands right in front of me, hands running up and down my arms comfortingly. "Thank you for allowing me to be part of that. You are amazing, Iz." Then, she pulls me in for a hug. I am so glad she is here.

Henley and Parker have stepped back into opposite corners of the room, each sort of sulking, yet still proud of me. But there's no time for that. Valentina needs us.

"Guys. We got to move. Now."

I start to explain what I learned, but I am still processing it. I reluctantly tell the gang what spell Mr. Hunting is trying to cast, and tell them that it is happening tonight. The sun is already starting to go down, we're running out of time.

I try to avoid eye contact with Henley but fail.

His eyes are full of fear and worry; probably reflecting my own. If I die tonight, I may never come back. He may finally lose me.

I reach out to him mentally, wanting to know his thoughts. But he blocks me. I look over at him, a little hurt and questioning.

He meets my eye and shakes his head sadly, not wanting me to know whatever is going through his mind.

Maybe I don't want to know either.

CHAPTER 9

ZACH'S VIEW

I turn away from the only girl I have ever loved, not wanting to see the disappointment in her eyes.

I just can't let her see what is going through my head.

Death. Lots of it. I can't stop it. It's a never ending reel of every single time Isabel has ever died in my arms.

The flashes keep going. She may be a little different, but her soul is the same every time. I always feel as though I die with her, but I don't. I never truly die, I just start over, waiting for her to find me, or me find her.

But there is a time, when I feel her loss- and the only thing that keeps me going to start over is the thought she always comes back to me.

But if Parker's father gets his way...I will lose her forever.

I sneak a glance at her, still blocking my thoughts. She is with the others, preparing for tonight. We leave soon.

I have loved every iteration of her, but this life she is the most different. Very stubborn. I chuckle to myself, not able to fully silence it.

Parker catches my eye. He knows I am thinking of our girl. But when am I not?

He walks over to me, grabbing my arm and pulling me into the corner, away from the others.

"Dude. I'm gonna need you to get it together. I can tell you're a wreck, and if the guy you hate most can tell, so can she." He says to me in a hushed tone. Looking back over his shoulder at the girl we both love.

"She is strong. I know she hasn't touched the full extent of her powers, but from what I know of witches, she is powerful, right?"

I nod. This version of Isabel is probably the most powerful, the original Isabel herself even thinks so I believe. They remind me a lot of one another. To have only known of her powers for one year and be able to levitate objects, read minds, clear intuition, and now the fact she can travel mentally over long distances...I know I can't do that.

But she has always been more powerful than me- I am just more patient and have the experience she doesn't realize she has.

Because I get to remember. She forgets. I always hope each life its changed, and that she will recognize me. But she never does.

In this life, I waited to make myself known. I found her while she was still in high school; discovering she had no idea she was a witch. She didn't have much relationship with her family, other than a long gone grandmother, and her true family was her best friend, Nicole.

I was content to watch her, until I knew she was ready to meet me. I've discovered from past mistakes it's easier to accept 'us' if she knows we are magical.

So I waited. Missing out valuable time on meeting the love of my lives. But I couldn't wait any longer when I realized Parker was hunting her.

His family has hunted us for generations, and when I realized who he was, I had to meet her. To tell her everything.

But that first time, I just wanted to be normal for her. So I avoided the big stuff and tried to get to know this version of her. Of course, everything she told me I already knew from watching her. But she *wanted* me to know her. I knew she could sense how right we were, she just didn't understand it. Then the hunter had to go screw it up.

I sigh. He's not so bad, at least not like his family.

He pulls me back to the present- "You okay, man?"

"Yes." I pull away, knowing Isabel is itching to leave. I feel the guilt radiating off of her from a room away. She is worried about Valentina. I am too.

"And Hunting- I don't hate you." I walk back in, sensing his surprise behind me.

I smirk. I do like to keep him on his toes though. With a quick wave of my hand, I send a rush of magic and close the door on his face. Even with the door closed, I still hear him cursing my name.

Everyone turns my way, shocked. I shrug, a small smile on my face.

Isabel looks at me, mouth agape. "Did you just-ugh. Oh my god." She rushes to the door, and swipes her hand the opposite direction, opening the door. Hunting stands there, fuming at me, hands in fists.

"Guys- can we focus please?" She says, shaking her head. But even she cannot hide the smile I see on her beautiful face. I knew she needed that.

She is about to face the possibility of death-both her own and Valentina's. The whole group needed a bit of a laugh, and I was happy to use Hunting to provide it.

I clap him on the back with a little more force than necessary, big ass smile on my face. "Ready to hunt?"

He glares back at me, before cracking a grin right back-
"Ready, witch."

CHAPTER 10

REALITY BITES.

The whole drive over I am silent. Both Nicole and Parker try to break the tension, but I am too lost in my own thoughts to participate.

I can't think of myself here. I need to make sure Valentina and all my friends make it out. I know Zach and Parker think differently, and probably the rest of them do too. They think I can live through the night. But I don't matter, not with this.

Valentina and everyone else is here because of me. Parker's dad has a personal vendetta against my existence, and we wouldn't be in this situation if it wasn't for me.

Once I'm gone, everyone's lives will be so much easier.

Nicole grabs my hand- "Stop it. I know what you're doing. Just stop it. Stop acting like you're already dead. That is not happening." I look down at her hand clutching mine. Then go to meet her brown eyes, tears wetting her long lashes.

"Please, Bel." *I can't lose you.*

I squeeze her hand back. It's weird to me-she seems to need me just as much as I need her. She has been the one constant in my life and when I thought I lost her friendship, I felt as though I lost my whole heart. She fears the same thing about me, I guess. She has always been the bright light in my sky, I always just felt lucky to be shined on by her.

You are my family, Bel. I don't care about these boys and their soulmate bullshit. You are my soulmate.

I smiled, tears starting to match hers. I pull her hand up to my mouth and give her a peck. I can't give her words to show her how much I love her, so I just keep ahold of her hand.

Liz looks over at us, a small smile on her face as she reaches over and puts her hand over ours.

"Sorry to interrupt, ladies. But we're here." Parker looks back from the driver's seat of his truck and we all let go, determined looks on all of our faces.

Zach gets out first and opens up his door, letting us all out of the back seat. We climb out, Parker and Zach waiting on us.

"First thing- we need to figure out where they are in the casting. Look around the room, pay attention to surroundings, but be careful." Zach looks at me wearily before continuing.

"So, if the spell has already been cast, then we need to make sure we get Isabel out of harm's way." He finishes, with Parker and the rest of the gang nodding in agreement.

"Fuck that." I say, cutting anyone off as they all look over at me in surprise. "My life does not hold more value than any other soul, any of yours or Valentina's. The priority is getting her out safely, that's all."

I take a breath before continuing, knowing this next part, as hard as it is on me, is even harder on them.

"I may die. Shhh don't interrupt Nic. I may die, and you all are just going to have to accept that. I have. But if you try to save me, and in the process hurt yourself or fail to save Valentina, you bet your soul I will come back to haunt you." I give each of them a look, ending with Zach. His eyes full of sadness, but even he nods back at me.

"Okay gang…who is ready to hunt a hunter?" Parker smiles wickedly.

He already schooled us on the way down on the factory. He has never been, but he knows how his dad operates. There will be some security that we will have to sneak through, probably his idiot brother, and then Valentina will be kept most likely in the basement. Which adds up to my dampness in the vision.

The location spell led us to this area, but it was my description that got us to this specific factory. Pretty cool.

I close my eyes, knowing I can do more. I feel her.

I feel Valentina, that means she is still alive!

I keep my eyes closed, trying to feel for mental presences. Parker was right. I only sense two minds- both dark, but one who's soul is black as night. Mr. Hunting.

"Hyde is close." I tell the others as we slowly creep to the entrance of the factory.

"I got this". Liz flashes a grin before pulling a stun gun out of her back pocket. What the heck?

I barely have time to react before she runs into the building and down the hall. I want to scream at her, tell her it's not safe, to wait for us, but she is already gone.

We all look at one another, before hurriedly following after her.

We finally catch up, a bit out of breath...at least I am... I don't run, okay? I power walk like nobody's business though.

Liz is crouched by a corner and uses hand signals to us before slowly creeping to the next hall. Me and Nicole look at each other and shrug before following our friend.

Parker and Zach head up the tail, wanting to round up our rag tag bunch.

Liz's hand signals start up again, this time more urgent. I crane my neck to see what she is gesturing to and see Hyde Hunting- Parker's son of a bitch brother. He looks like Parker in many ways, but rougher, like he hasn't had it easy. Parker has taken his life and found something to smile at, but if Hyde smiled at me, I think it would only be if he was causing me pain.

He had a barn fall on him a few months ago thanks to Nicole slamming Parker's truck into it, and I heard he was hospitalized for a while. But he seemed to be back to normal, huge and menacing just like before.

He stretches his neck from right to left, causing a loud crack. He moaned after the release of tension, and the noise sent a shiver up my spine. I turn back to look at Parker and he is silencing gagging. Then he smiles and me shrugging as if to say, 'you can't choose your family.' But I did. I chose Liz, Nicole, him, and Zach as my family, even Valentina and of course Puff. Thinking of Puff, I reach for the brecciated jasper still in my pocket from the location spell. I know it's crazy, but I wish that little ball of fur was here. She always makes me feel calm and right. Zach does too, but with him I never can tell if it's me or my soul feeling the rightness.

Liz looks back at us, giving up on the hand signals, I think finally getting we don't have a clue what she's saying. She mouths, "I need to get closer" and waves the stun gun as if we forgot.

We all look back in shock but when she moves closer to Hyde, Parker has to hold me and Nicole back.

Zach whispers, "I think she knows what she's doing…and if she doesn't we're right here. But give her a chance." We relax, and I sink in to Parker's arms a little longer than I should as we wait to see Liz's plan unfold.

She stays low as she creeps closer to Hyde. He clearly is not who should be on guard. He seems like he is barely awake.

His back is turned to her, but a piece of glass crunching underneath her feet makes us all freeze.

Hyde whips around, anger and confusion flashes across his face. He takes a step toward Liz, reaching his huge arms towards her. She clicks a button and the stun gun shoots a line at him, immobilizing him in his tracks.

I watch as the shocks tear through his body, stiffening up all of his muscles before bringing his giant self to the hard floor.

"Gotta say- I didn't hate seeing that, Liz." Parker claps a hand on my friend's back. Zachary walks past her, back to his mission, but gives her a small smile in congratulations.

Nicole then goes by, whispering, "Badass." Liz giggles, then starts to follow the rest of them.

I can't seem to take my eyes off of Hyde. It's crazy how someone can look so much like Parker, but be so different. I start to reach for his mind, curiosity getting the better of me.

Just like Parker, his life has not been easy. Same impossible expectations, but things didn't come easy to him like they did Parker. Hyde thought that when Parker soiled on the legacy, his father would embrace him with open arms. But that didn't happen.

He just started beating him harder, and asking Hyde to do impossible things. Hyde always liked the dark side, but his father was evil in a way he could never be. Maybe if he could kill me his father would finally be proud of him.

Wait, what?

I was so lost in his head, I didn't realize he was waking up. He reached his hand and grabbed my ankle, causing me to lose my footing and go to the ground. My knees slicing into the cracked glass on the factory floor. I wince and try to break myself free, try to persuade him mentally, but the pain of the glass embedded in my knee is making it hard to think.

He smiles, knowing he's got me. Then a flash of white goes across my peripheral vision. I shake my head, trying to clear the pain. I must be seeing things.

I hear a loud *meoww,* and that was the only warning I get before Puff lands on Hyde's neck, slicing in with her paws right into his jugular. She clamps down with her paws and then bites down, *hard.* He thrashes about, but he lets go of my ankle. I scoot away and reach out with my hands forcefully. His head slams back, Puff jumping off before his head could hit the ground, knocking him out.

Puff slowly walks over to me, casually like she didn't just attack a 250 lb man.

She sits and glares at me. I take out the crystal in my pocket and look at it in shock.

I reach for her and she bites my hand, gentle, like when she first met me. Blood still wells up where her teeth broke the skin.

She laps at the wound with her scratchy tongue then moves on to my slashed up knees.

The wounds heal, and she starts to leave, knowing her job is done.

"Puff...can you understand me?"

Always have, human. Now, try not to die. I would hate to start over with someone else.

"I love you too, Puff."

CHAPTER 11

THE FINAL ONE.

I catch up to the gang. They had just turned around to find me, thinking I was with them the whole time.

"You okay, Iz?" Henley questioned, eyebrows raised, taking me in, checking for anything wrong. But he won't find anything, Puff made sure of that.

"Thanks to Puff I am." I smile back at them, a little mad at myself for my curiosity getting the better of me when it came to Hyde.

I go to Parker as the others continue on, pulling him back.

"I need you to hear this and believe it- I am amazed by the man you are. You are nothing like your family, and in case you didn't know, I am so proud of you." I squeeze his arm, shock filling his eyes, and I follow our friends, not giving any explanation at my sudden outburst.

I race back towards the group, squeezing Henley's arm, as I catch up to him. *Thank you. For everything. I know I was reluctant to join your world but now I can't imagine me without being a witch.* *You saved me.* I send over to him with a smile. He looks over at me, a question in his eye. Then he sighs and projects: *I've never been good at saying goodbye to you, and I am not starting now. Let's go, Isabel.* Then, he quickened his pace, heading towards the dark creepy stairs of the basement.

We stop just short of the door, aware of the danger awaiting us downstairs. We need to find out where they are in the spell, save Valentina, but there is not good recon spot for a basement. We just have to blindly walk in.

I look back at Parker, he's trying to focus up after the shock statement i gave him earlier. He then moves to the front of us. A decision made in his mind- "Wait a bit, then follow down after me. He is my dad."

I sense his resolve and though I want to go down with him, be there for him now; I give him his space.

Parker's POV

I know what she's doing. But that shit is not gonna fly. If anyone is going to act all self sacrificing, it's gonna be me. If I am everything she says I am, good and all that, why wouldn't it be me to do this?

That's what good people do; they go down the scary stairs of death first and try to subdue their dad before the people they love get hurt. Right?

I look behind making sure they're not following me. Not yet anyways. I curse every creak the stairs make, also why are there creaky stairs in an abandoned factory? I am very sure these are the stairs of death and this floor is the murder floor. They would go down here to murder the workers who screwed up putting on the toothpaste caps or whatever this factory made. I can totally see it.

I also can feel it. This place is dark. I may not have powers like Zachary or Isabel, but the deeper I go on these stairs, the more dark energy I feel.

I am only three steps away from the bottom, and it still is pretty dark everywhere.   No sign of the Valentina chick and worse- no sign of dad.

Maybe Hyde was here just to slow us down…maybe we're too late…I turn back, about to rush up to tell the rest of the group. To tell them we need to wrap Isabel in bubble wrap and ship her to Antarctica where no one will ever hurt her.

"Hello, devil boy…Come to see dear ole dad?" I slowly turn around at the voice that has haunted me my whole life.

My dad is there, smiling at me an evil grin at the bottom of the stairs, appearing out of nowhere. Valentina is slumped against the wall closest to him, clutching the book. They must have cast some concealment spell, because I swear they weren't there a minute ago. She doesn't look like she can move that much right now anyways.

I turn, wanting to warn them, seeing in my peripheral Dad swinging back something. I brace my body, knowing pain is heading straight towards me..

He's coming for you. I send Isabel before everything all goes black.

Parker was gone maybe two minutes when we heard the thump. Right before, I swear I heard his voice warning me.

I push my way forward and peek down the staircase, just in time to see his large body crash towards the floor. Then... it disappeared.

"Concealment spell. We are walking in blind." I hear Zach curse under his breath. I reach for his hand with one hand and Nicole's with the other. He grabs ahold of Liz with his free hand.

"So let's change that, shall we?" I look to each of them, before concentrating on seeing through the dark. I know they're down there- I just need to see it. The spell was cast by him, with Valentina's guidance, so I could see its weakness. We just were taken surprise by it- but we're ready now.

I focus on the right path, my power of intuition should help clear the spell. Though I feel their hands gripping mine, my friends start to go blurry and everything at the bottom starts to get clearer.

I see Parker sitting against a wall, passed out. Valentina standing right by him, clutching the spell book, and Mr. Hunting standing at the bottom step waiting for us, big cocky grin on his face.

I let go of my friend's hands and run down, needing to save Parker and Valentina from the crazy man eyeing me down like I am a prime rib special. I hear everyone following me, I sense their apprehension.

I send out my mind to Mr. Hunting's and say *Look behind you*. He whips around, expecting an attack from behind.

I use the distraction to shoot past him down the stairs. Straight to Valentina and the book.

He curses and walks towards me, a knife appearing in his hand.

"You are just in time, devil girl. You see, the spell you and lover boy cast was enforced with blood and love. I don't have the love." I spare a glance at Parker slumped on the floor, starting to come to. But I see a nasty welp on the side of his head from being knocked out. I look over at the rest of my friends coming around the other side to try to surround Parker's dad. I sense Zach building up his powers, I just need to distract Mr. Hunting. Then, maybe we both can get everyone out.

"Sounds like you don't have much to work with then." He growls and I see the hand holding the knife start to shake, as if he is itching to use it on me. Maybe that should be the plan then. Goad him into slicing into me before the spell is cast, then everyone would have time to act. Most people would get out alive. I just may be alive a little later than them...

"For me, I have to use blood to power up the spells. I have been using your friend's here," He gestures to Valentina, and now I see it. The slices down her leg, he was blood letting her for spells. Using her own blood against her, and not letting her heal with the weakening spell.

"I see not only did you bring yourself to me, ready for the kill, but you brought so many more blood bags for me to use." He smiled again, and it is nothing like Parker. It is evil and full of hate. While Parker's is mischievous, he has so much good you can see it every time he grins.

This man plans to hurt my friends. He is waving a knife in my face, trying to scare me. It's working. But I am a bad ass witch. He is just a man.

I grab the book from Valentina and run towards my friends, trying to shield them, or at least give Zach a good distraction. He has been building up his powers this whole time. I sneak a glance over to him, seeing his hands tense and starting to shake.

Then, Parker's dad is thrown up into the air. Hovering for a minute, before being slammed back into the ground.

Woah. I look over at Zach, his breathing heavy, exactly as if he just lifted a man up into the air. Huh. That's kinda hot. Am I weird for saying that?

We run over to Valentina and Parker, Zach staying were he is to keep Mr. Hunting form getting back up.

Liz and Nicole go to Parker, each taking an arm and hoisting him up. Leading him towards the stairs, back to freedom.

I go to Valentina, who after letting go of the book, has completely slumped to the floor.

"We're here, we made it. Just come on- we can get out here and heal you." The words come out quickly, my hands going underneath her arms to help her up.

She swats my hands away, though with no real force behind it. "Do you remember what I asked you the very first day we met?" She said weakly, her eyes bearing into my soul.

"Um, can we talk about this later…" I look over at Zach as his hands are shaking, struggling to keep Hunting down.

Valentina puts her hand on my face, cupping her cheek. I see so many more cuts than before, all over her body. We need to heal her fast. She has lost so much blood.

"Think, my dear. I asked you a question." So I think. I think back to that very first day. Feeling so out of place, thinking Valentina was a kooky woman, she is, but she is so much more to me now. I remember I needed something for my dreams…what was it she asked me…

"Am I ready for what's to come?" I answer her, voice shaking.

"Yes. You weren't then. But I always was. I knew it would come to this. You and me- we were meant to meet. I was meant to guide you.   Now, you will be ready for anything." With each word, her voice goes quieter, me straining to hear. Her hand slips from my face, and she slides back down to the floor.

"No! Zach, Valentina, she's-" I turn sharply to Zach needing his help, and I see he is now on his knees, with a knife at his throat. Mr. Hunting is holding the knife, smiling triumphantly.

"So we can't use her blood anymore I see. You know what will work even better? The blood of the two original casters. That will make it binding.

I see the knife start to lean in deeper to Henley's skin of his neck, little beads of blood dripping down. I freeze, knowing any sudden movements will result in his death.

"Good- now grab the book." Hunting jeers at me, nodding his head over the book I had dripped to care for Valentina. Oh Valentina. I glance over and see her eyes have closed. I squish down a sob, not wanting him to hear he has won.

I reach down for the book, careful not to jostle Valentina, as it looks as though she is only resting. A tear slides down my face, right as my hands touch the book.

Claim it. I look up sharply, wondering where the voice had come from.

I see me. The original me. I stifle a gasp. Never have my visions blended so much into real life. It looked almost as if a ghost was watching over me.

I glance over Hunting, knife still raised at Henley's throat, not freaking out over my doppelgänger. He can't see her- I sigh a small breath of relief. But I see Henley's eyes go wide- He can see her too.

Hands still on the book, I look to where Henley's eyes went. Expecting to see just the original me once more.

I cannot hide the gasp that comes from my body.

Every single iteration of me stands before me.

Whispers come at me from all directions. Eyes staring into me, willing me to listen.

Claim it. Claim it for yourself. Claim thyself.

Claim yourself.

"Go ahead. Open it, witch." Hunting sneered at me, unaware of the full on battalion settling around him. I looked at each of them, begging them to help. Then I hear their incessant plea again- *Claim it.*

I put my hands over the book, spreading my fingers wide. The book knows exactly what to do, opening and going to the page of my and Zachary's original spell. It had been transcribed years later, but I could see, that just copying instructions would not do what it did to us.

You had to have the love behind the words.

I look up at the stairs, seeing movement. Parker is on his feet again, shock rippling through his face. Liz and Nicole stand on either side of him, their mouths falling open.

I send a small smile at them, hoping they know. I love them all.

I then look back over to Zach, who is still in shock over all the different Isabel's before him. I know he can't help me out of this. No one can. But me.

"I know what to do, Hunter." I won't call him the same name as Parker, I just won't do it.

"I will cast the spell, breaking the original one." I hear Nicole gasp from the stairs. Always for the dramatics, my best friend.

I continue- "Since I am the one casting, and not you, I don't need blood. So you can put away the knife." I gesture over at Zach, hoping he will release him.

'No, no, no. I will do no such thing. This knife is the only thing keeping your friends and my son from running down and it's your incentive to cast this spell."

Is it?

I look around- Liz...thrust into this world and she was embracing it, just out of support for me. I love her.

Nicole...I feel as though she may be more part of this world than she realizes, but she stands by my side and is there for me always, no matter what. I love my best friend.

Parker...I feel his guilt, I feel his desire to come and save us. But he can't- he makes one move down and Zach's neck gets sliced. We all know it. I know he hunted me- but I think the fact he has come so far and made me his own personal vendetta only makes me love him more. I love Parker.

Finally... Zachary Henley. How must he feel seeing all of me before him? Losing us all at once? But he risks it every time. He could have broken the spell long ago if he just made the choice to not meet me. But he chose me time and time again. Just a little of time with me in each life was worth all the heartbreak that came with loving me. I love him.

"Stop dawdling and get to it, witch." I see more drops of blood go down Zach's neck.

I need to do this, now.

I think of all the love I have around me. I think of all the Isabels surrounding me. The original Isabel didn't have what I have, her and Zach only had each other. I have that and so much more. I feel everyone's love strengthening me, I feel the Isabels support around me. I hear them, guiding me what to do next. *Claim it.*

I drop my hands to the book and close my eyes. I see it- I see when Isabel and Zachary cast the spell. They held hands and embraced, an unseen force binding them together. They didn't know at the time... but it was for forever.

My hands start to shake, this isn't something I can just read from the book. If Hunting would have cast this, it wouldn't have been done right. But I will do this. I will finish this once and for all.

I look up at Zach; *I'm sorry. I can't lose you, even if it means losing us.* If he didn't have a knife to his throat, he would have nodded. He understands. He always does.

My hands remain over the book, still shaking with the built up power, the love I have been siphoning into them.

Claim it.

So I do.

I slice my hands open, cutting the binds between all of me and Zach, breaking the spell that lasted lifetimes. Our souls no longer bound, I hear all of the past me's take a breath, then I feel them fade away.

I sway with the loss I just dealt. I feel as though a part of my soul is gone, as if I just carved out a piece of my heart.

Hunter releases the knife from Henley's throat, moving with eagerness to me. Henley falls to the floor, weak from the spell that broke our binds.

I know I am about to die. Hunter, in his excitement, drops the knife and wraps his hands around my throat. Because of what I just did, Hunter can now kill me. Nicole, Liz, and Parker rush down the stairs. Maybe to save me, maybe to check on Zach. But they will be too late. For me anyways. It doesn't matter what Parker's dad does to me now. Because even if I am the one who signed my death certificate, I chose it. I claimed myself. No fate has any power over me now. I control myself.

Hearing that changes something in me. I will not let this man kill my friends. I may die, but he doesn't get to make that choice for me or for them.

The oxygen is leaving my body, I know I don't have much time left. But I think back to all of my dreams, and how Parker's ancestors would do the very same thing to me. Every time they would kill me, I would come back, spoiling their plans. I won't be able to come back this time. But I will take him down with me.

My hands were clutching at his, trying to pry them from my throat. But I move them to his throat. I think of how the oxygen is leaving my body. I think of all that this man and his family has done to the people I care about... and to me.

I imagine the same breath that is leaving my body start to leave his. His hands start to loosen on my throat, still constricting but not as much. It's been too long though, I know I don't have much time left.

I feel sorry for you old man. Even with all of this, you still won't win. Even if I die, you will still be an old man with no one to love him. I have so much more than you will ever have.

I send to him my final thoughts, using my last strength to pull every ounce of breath from his body.

I feel his hands leave my throat, I let a small smile, knowing he can't hurt my friends.

I can rest now.

The smile is still on my face when I hit the floor.

CHAPTER 12

AFTER.

So this is it. Death. My soul has never really experienced this. Every time I wished for peace, I was reset, starting over another life.

I remember now. The spell broke and all the memories came rushing back. I remember every single moment I shared with Zach. I remember the love I felt for him and how I wanted to share everything with him.

But I also still remember Nicole. Her protecting me growing up. I remember when I started my period and she gave me her jacket and personally escorted me to the nurse. Verbally threatening anyone who looked at me funny. Her bringing me tea whenever she knew it was a tough day. I could really use some right now. Does heaven have tea? Is this heaven?

I remember Liz. How even though she came into my life late, she made such an impact on me immediately. She quietly forged her place in my life and made herself irreplaceable. She never pushed me past my limits, but also knew I could do more than what I thought of myself.

Parker. I remember every touch. Every shiver that was sent up my spine. I always thought it was the witch in me that caused my body to react against him. But it was the bond between Zach and me. It rejected anyone who would have threatened it. I see that now. My body was reacting to the spell, but instead of pushing me away, I still found my way in his arms.

I remember them all. I remember Puff and hope someone takes over feeding her. Though I feel like she is more than capable of taking care of herself. I want her to have love.

I want them all to have love.

I made it past finding out I was a witch, getting kidnapped, survived and understood my dreams, met my past lives, survived the void of my mind, and learned to harness my powers to save all of my friends.

So why do I feel like I still have more to do?

Because you're not dead, idiot human. Open your eyes.

Puff? Wait, what? Is Puff in heaven?

"Isabel, honey, wake up." Liz's voice cuts through the fog.

"Bel, you better wake up or I am going to kick your-" Nicole couldn't just let me die in peace, could she?

I feel strong hands wrap around mine. I then feel gentle fingers run across my cheek. My boys.

I'm alive?

I open my eyes and see everyone around me, even Puff. Worried looks on their faces, quickly turning to relief. Well, except Puff, she looks pretty much the same, except maybe a bit annoyed.

"Is everyone okay?" I croak out. I did just get choked out by a crazy person.

"Yes, Isabel Grace. Everyone is okay, thanks to you." Parker squeezes my hand. "Even my dad is alive, though I think you may have been too easy on him. He is passed out and the police are coming to pick him up. We can finally get him for some of the evil he has done."

I look over at Valentina's body, still against the wall. I let out a sob. I didn't save everyone.

Zach pulls me up wrapping me in his arms. "She is so proud of you, Iz. You claimed yourself. You freed yourself... you freed me." He is a bit broken still, but he now has the freedom to make his own choices, finally after years of fate guiding him.

"But...this is our last life, right?"

Nicole pulls me out of Zach's arms, helping me to my feet. "Yeah, welcome to how the rest of the world lives, guys."

I smile at each of them. I have the power of choice now. I give Zach and Parker each a small smile, before grabbing Liz and Nicole's hands. I lead them up the stairs.

"Who is up for some food? I know a really good cafe that is always open." I hear Zach chuckle behind me. Liz and Nicole shake their heads with a smile, and Parker and Zach stay behind, ready to send Mr. Hunting to where he belongs. They will meet us there- they know where to go. I smile and walk on, ready for what is to come.

This is my final life.

Better make it count.

A Little Down the Road...

Puff gazed over at her human. All of the others are here as well, taking over her home.

The overly affectionate neighbor that would sneak her treats when Isabel wasn't looking. The quiet one who gave the best pets... not that Puff would let her know that.

Then there were the males that seemed to never leave her human alone. The loud and big one, always finding an excuse to touch Isabel and the one who always smiles at her. He has tried to communicate with Puff, but she would never allow that. She barely lets her own human talk with her.

They are all crowded around the apartment living room, cheering Isabel on as she practices her latest spells. As long as they don't try to levitate her, Puff will let them be. Seems like Isabel is maybe getting the hang of the whole witch thing. Finally.

Puff licks her paw and looks at the humans from her safe space, the cushion on the floor of the living room facing the sun. Rubbing her paw against her ear, and silently wishing someone will notice her and give some pets. It certainly won't be the Parker fellow. He only ever has eyes for her human. The other witch isn't much help either, caught between wanting to help Isabel with her magic, and not crossing the new line that is between them. It is different than before, but there is still something connecting the three.

Puff lets out what only can be described as a sigh. However it comes out like, "Meorrrw." It is enough to get the attention of the quiet friend though, and the one who has powers laying dormant for the time being. Some may wonder what powers she may have, or maybe some may ponder who will her human end up with with no fate deciding it for her?

But Puff simply does not care.

From the arms of the calm friend, who Puff has allowed to carry her, Puff once again gazes at her human who has caused her so much trouble in her short life as a familiar.

Isabel is laughing, dark blonde hair loosely hanging on her shoulders, and looking brightly at her friends surrounding her. The light shines across her striking eyes, making them sparkle. She is free. She is happy. That is enough for Puff.

Now...if only she would stop buying Puff dry kibble.

AUTHOR'S NOTE

I started Isabel's journey over ten years ago. I was finishing up college at the time, and made anyone who would listen read my first drafts.

Now, I am a wife, and a mom, and while I have always written, I never called myself a writer. It wasn't until I had the encouragement from my friends and family to just publish the dang thing.

Dreams did have a lot of errors throughout, though it also had a lot of heart I like to say. I was so eager to get it done, as it had been such a long time coming. Isabel has always felt like a huge piece of me, and getting to tell her story felt a bit like exposing my heart to the world.

Nightmares only took me about a month to write. Isabel was pushing me to get the rest of her story out, and I was happy to oblige. It was like the words poured out of me. If Dreams was my heart, Nightmares was my soul. But something felt different writing going into book two, Isabel was starting to grow up and so were her friends.

Although I feel like this book, Reality, was my best one I have written, it was at times the hardest to write. I knew Isabel's story was coming to an end. She grew up, just like I did, and it was time for this chapter to close. I kept putting off writing the final chapter, not quite ready to say goodbye.

I am not sure how the ending will be perceived honestly, because I didn't choose Team Parker or Team Henley. I chose Isabel. That is where I hesitate to call this a romance; it was never about them, it always was about her.

Who knows what choices Isabel will make now that she is free? I may have my guesses...but I am not telling.

When it comes down to it though, this last book was about the relationships with Isabel's found family. Fun fact, Isabel is based off of me, and her friends are based on real life people. Nicole is a mix of my childhood best friends, who still are there for me at the drop of a hat. Liz is a mix of two best friends I made in adulthood, two of the kindest, smartest women I know. Valentina is named after another best friend, who is a witch in her own way I fully believe. Finally, Parker and Henley's very best traits are inspired by my knight in shining armor, my husband.

Isabel's story may be done (for now at least), but I have more ideas in my head waiting to come to life. I hope you will stick around and enjoy the ride. Just like Isabel, you never know what magic could be waiting for you.

Before I go, I just wanted to say thank you. Thank you to Sheena, who not only inspired a character, was my editor, but was the biggest push and loudest supporter. My friends, who read my book back when it was just three chapters (I am looking at you Ali) and have supported me through every step of the way. Every market, every signing, every supportive text pushing me to keep going. I can't even describe the joy I had when I had a friend message me whenever she read each book giving me updates and thoughts, even telling me she laughed out loud.

I like to think I am funny, but it was nice to be vindicated.

Lastly, I would like to thank my family. My brother was one of the ones who inspired me to write. He is so creative and his ideas could create entire worlds. Thank you to my sister and brother and sister in law, who fought the heat and rain to support my endeavors. Thank you to my mom and dad, who believed my sociology degree and a lifetime of training in dance, could somehow achieve author status. But honestly, even with all of their jokes, they have always been my biggest cheerleaders. My daughter, who has not read my book, but pushed me to fight for my dreams so one day she can fight for hers. My husband, who I feel like is playing the longest game of improv with me. I spout crazy ideas, and he smiles and says, "Yes, and...". Never a doubt in his mind that I could do whatever I wanted to do. Pursue education? Change careers? Self publish three books? Decide I really want to 'do' the author thing and drag him to every market and reader's fest around the state? "Yes, and...". He puts our family's needs first and has put his dreams aside to support mine. You're next, babe.

Love you all. Thanks for listening to my rants and visions.

ABOUT THE AUTHOR

BETHANY PHELPS LEPRETRE

Dance teacher and Director by day, book author by night, Bethany certainly likes to stay busy. Bethany has always loved reading and writing, and journaled every event growing up and into adulthood. Her wedding vows were full of journal entries documenting her relationship. While reading and writing has always been a huge part of her life, only recently did she decide to pursue it by self publishing her three books.

Her first, "Dreams:A Peek into the Past" was a work of heart that she had slowly chipped away at for years before deciding to take the plunge and publish. Her next book, the sequel, "Nightmares: Further into the Future", only took about a month to write. Finishing the trilogy the very next summer with "Reality", Bethany cannot wait for what is next on her author journey and is so excited of what is to come.

Bethany loves the beach, reading, and spending time with her family. Bethany lives in Seabrook with her husband Kegan, their daughter Livvy, and their two dogs, Traeger and Stella.